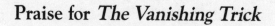

Praise for *The Vanishing Trick*

'A thrilling, evocative and eerie tale – I adored it!'
Michelle Harrison, author of *A Pinch of Magic*

'An eventful gothic adventure full of secrets and surprises'
Sunday Times Book of the Week

'Ghosts, gadgets, likeable villains and unlikely heroes –
dark and dazzling adventure' Emma Carroll, author of
Letters from the Lighthouse

'[A] superlative debut ... atmospheric and
transporting' *Guardian*

'A gripping and vivid Victorian tale with a wickedly
unforgettable villain' Anna Fargher, author of
The Umbrella Mouse

'A completely enthralling tale, oozing with atmosphere and
originality' Catherine Doyle, author of
The Stormkeeper's Island

'Deliciously dark and atmospheric ... I couldn't get enough'
Nizrana Farook, author of *The Girl Who Stole an Elephant*

THE INCREDIBLE TALKING MACHINE

Jenni Spangler

SIMON & SCHUSTER

First published in Great Britain in 2021 by Simon & Schuster UK Ltd

Text copyright © 2021 Jenni Spangler
Illustrations copyright © 2021 Chris Mould

1 3 5 7 9 10 8 6 4 2

Simon & Schuster UK Ltd
1st Floor, 222 Gray's Inn Road
London WC1X 8HB

www.simonandschuster.co.uk
www.simonandschuster.com.au
www.simonandschuster.co.in

Simon & Schuster Australia, Sydney
Simon & Schuster India, New Delhi

A CIP catalogue record for this book is available from the British Library.

PB ISBN 978-1-4711-9039-1
eBook ISBN 978-1-4711-9040-7
eAudio ISBN 978-1-4711-9988-2

Printed and bound by CPI Group (UK) Ltd, Croydon, CR0 4YY

MIX
Paper from
responsible sources
FSC® C020471

MANCHESTER'S THEATRE ROYALE

Home of all things spectacular and wondrous

PRESENTS

THE INCREDIBLE TALKING MACHINE!

All the way from Vienna

Be Astonished! Amazed! Astounded!

Professor Faber has created the impossible:
a device of wood and metal which

SPEAKS WITH A HUMAN VOICE

Of great interest to all with a mind for Scientific Knowledge and
those with a heart for amusement and delight

For the first time outside London and showing every evening
throughout July.

SHE SPEAKS! SHE LAUGHS! SHE SINGS!

Doors open at 6.30 p.m.

Private boxes available. Children half price.

Lights Up

All theatres are haunted.

Manchester's Theatre Royale was haunted by a dead opera singer known as Cold Annie. Actors complained of an icy, creeping dread whenever they used the dressing room that had once belonged to her, and stagehands avoided the places she was said to roam late at night. Rumour was that if she appeared before a performance, it was sure to go horribly wrong.

But Tig Rabbit wasn't scared.

She liked to imagine that Cold Annie simply loved the theatre, and had decided never to leave. Sometimes, when Tig was waiting alone in the dark to lift the curtains, or tidying the costumes away late at night, she had the sensation that Annie was nearby. It made her feel less lonely.

She'd mentioned this once to Gus, the carpenter's boy,

who was two years older and considered himself superior. This was a mistake. Ever since, he'd teased her about how stupid it was to believe in ghosts. Still, Tig noticed he never went into Annie's dressing room, and he was nowhere to be found when it was time to go into the dark auditorium to light or extinguish the lamps.

That was why, even though Gus was supposed to do it an hour ago, Tig was lighting the lamps herself. The new act would be here any moment, and they'd all be in trouble if the job wasn't done. Typical of Gus, the coward, to shirk his duties. She'd get him back for it.

In the blackness at the edge of the stage, she set her foot on the bottom rung of a ladder which stretched up, taller than a house, into the rigging above. The auditorium was so quiet Tig could hear the flicker of the tiny flame at the end of her long lamp-lighting stick. There were no windows in the cavernous room so although it was early afternoon dark stillness wrapped around her like a blanket, pushing against the feeble light.

Tig didn't mind. She could do this with her eyes closed. Carefully she climbed, one hand clutching the light-stick and the other keeping her balance on the rungs. Thirty-two steps to the flies, where long beams spanning the width of the stage held a complicated web of ropes and pulleys. Dizzyingly high, hidden from the sight of the audience – this was Tig's world.

Some days she felt like a ghost herself, inhabiting the secret in-between spaces of the Royale. She walked through the walls, crouched behind the scenery, crawled beneath the seats. If needed, she could travel from basement to roof without being seen by a single living soul. It made her feel like she belonged, that she was a small part of the theatre magic – that she was home. A home full of long hours and hard work and a frustrating boss, a home very different to the one she had lived in before her father died, but a home all the same.

Reaching the top of the ladder, she pulled herself up onto a narrow walkway, holding the light-stick ahead of her as she found her footing.

The stage lights were the pride of the Royale. New-fangled gas lamps – the first theatre in Manchester to install them. They were brighter, and far easier, than lighting the place with candles, but there was a knack to it. There were two rows of five lamps – one at each side of the stage. Tig leaned over the edge of the walkway and used the clover-shaped hook on the end of the light-stick to twist the valve, allowing gas to flow down the long, shiny pipes and ooze out of each lamp.

Now she had to be fast. She touched the flame of the light-stick to the top of the first lamp and with a pop and a flare of heat it burst into life. She ran to the next light. Pop. Two flames lit.

Every wasted second let gas seep into the air, the eggy sulphur smell warning Tig to act quickly. If too much gas escaped it might cause an explosion, and the whole theatre would go up in smoke. She ran along the line, her footsteps on the metal walkway echoing off the high ceiling, pausing briefly to light each lamp in turn.

One side done. Already the theatre was transformed. Warm, yellowish light washed over the stage and painted Tig's shadow as a giant on the wall behind her. The glow spilled out beyond the edge of the stage, catching the golden scrolls and vines that decorated the royal boxes and illuminating the first few rows of empty seats.

Her stomach fluttered with anticipation as she thought about the new performer who was arriving that day. Different to the usual acting troupes and opera singers, Professor Faber had come all the way from Vienna with his greatest invention – a machine that could speak with a human voice. The thought alone sent a shiver down Tig's spine. What could be more magical than that?

Now to light the other side. The proper thing to do next was to climb down, cross the stage, and go through the Green Room – the actors' waiting area. Inside was another ladder that led to the walkway and the gas valve for the other set of lights. But distant voices and a scuffling sound were coming from the front of the building. The professor must be here already! Mr Snell, the theatre manager, would be furious if the lights weren't lit. Tig would have to take a short cut across the girders.

Careful to keep the flame of the light-stick away from her clothes, she ducked under the railing and stepped out onto one of the narrow metal beams that reached right across the

4

stage. A glance down at the hard boards far below made Tig feel queasy.

Walking across the girders was not allowed – it was much too dangerous, as one slip would be a disaster. But Tig knew she could do it, and there wasn't a second to waste.

Chin up. Eyes on the end of the beam. She held her light-stick horizontally with both hands, using it to guide her balance, just as she had seen the acrobats do on the tight-rope a few months before. One foot in front of the other. Step. Step. Step. Simple. She kept her eyes fixed on that one spot where the girder met the walkway on the opposite side and in a matter of seconds she was almost at the end. The air was cooler here, away from the burning lamps. She looked up.

Cold Annie.

Tig shivered as though she'd been doused in cold water. The ghost was standing on the walkway, right at the point Tig needed to climb through the railings. Tig's heart beat a little faster, and she gripped the light-stick tighter. Of course she wasn't *afraid* of Annie, but a ghost is a ghost, and Tig had never seen her so clearly, or so close, before.

She was a slight figure, older than Tig but not much bigger, dressed in a high-waisted gown. She wasn't white or see-through as ghosts were often described, but a soft milky blue, hair, face and clothes alike. She appeared solid enough that Tig might bump into her, but the wall behind her showed only Tig's shadow. Annie's left eye was bright and sharp and fixed on Tig, but the right eye looked closed. No – it was missing, the eyelid sunk back a little way into her head.

5

The ghost made no sound but tilted her head to the right and squinted, as if wondering who Tig was.

'I'm lighting—' Tig's voice came out quiet and cracked. She swallowed hard. 'I'm lighting the lamps.'

Goosebumps rose on Tig's arms from the chill Annie radiated.

'I need to get past,' said Tig, suddenly remembering that she was very high up indeed, and balanced on a narrow beam, and that Mr Snell and the professor would be here any moment and the lamps weren't lit . . . 'Can I come up?'

For a second, it seemed Annie understood as she glided slightly backwards. Tig took a tentative step forward. Her hands shook, just a tiny bit, but she painted on a smile to show she was friend, not foe.

A bang.

The doors at the back corner of the stage had been flung open. They were here.

Tig held her breath. She couldn't stay here – it wouldn't take Snell long to notice only half the lights were lit and as soon as he looked up, she'd be caught. He'd be furious with her. Mr Snell believed children should be neither seen nor heard, and he didn't like them to interrupt while he was showing off to a new guest, either.

But Annie was still blocking her path. Tig nodded and waved at the ghost, urging her out of the way, but she didn't move.

Mr Snell emerged onto the stage, followed by two furniture movers buckling under the weight of something almost as big as a piano. It was wrapped tightly in woollen blankets held in place by thick straps.

The talking machine.

Tig was torn between keeping her eyes on Cold Annie and watching what was going on beneath her. She had been dreaming about the talking machine for weeks, ever since she'd heard it was coming, and couldn't bear to miss the first glimpse.

'Careful! Careful with her!' A fourth man followed the movers in. In contrast to their sturdy corduroy overalls and caps, this man wore a top hat and a black suit. 'Watch the legs!'

Professor Faber, surely. His accent was unfamiliar to Tig, the words angular and staccato.

'Gently!' The professor moved in quick, sharp gestures and shouted his instructions at the men, who looked thoroughly fed up of it. 'Lower to the ground very—'

They dropped their burden with a great thud and a metallic clang.

The professor groaned. 'Useless! Why do you send me such men?'

What was Tig going to do now? The talking machine was almost directly below her. Mr Snell would surely see.

'Thank you, gents,' said Snell, handing over some money to the movers, who scurried off as quickly as possible.

'Yes!' shouted the professor after them. 'Be gone, fools!'

'May I say what an absolute pleasure it is to have you at the Theatre Royale?' Snell cleared his throat and stepped forward, holding out his arm for a handshake.

'You may.' The professor ignored the handshake and walked directly to his machine. He began methodically unfastening the straps.

'I'm sure you'll be most happy here,' said Snell. 'Humble though it is.'

The professor stopped for a moment and glanced around. *Please don't look up!*

'It appears adequate.' He turned back to his machine.

That was close. Tig had to move now. The beam was too narrow to turn around, and besides, walking all the way back to the other side was risky – her footsteps might give her away.

'You have followed my instructions, yes?' said the professor. 'I have appropriate lodgings here in the theatre?'

'We've made up a bed for you in the Green Room.' Snell dabbed his forehead with a handkerchief. He always got sweaty when he was flustered, which was most of the time. 'Though I must say, it's most irregular, Mr Faber.'

'Professor.'

'Professor Faber, most of our guests prefer the comfort of the Golden Lion Hotel to—'

'The machine is too delicate to be dragged through the streets. I do not leave my machine; therefore, I do not leave the theatre.'

Tig swallowed hard and took another slow, small step towards Annie. Surely she would move – or perhaps Tig would pass right through her like smoke? Either way, Tig had little choice.

'The machine will be perfectly safe here in the theatre,' Snell continued to protest, his face now as red as the velvet curtains.

'Leave me now.' Faber gave a dismissive wave.

'Perhaps you'd like a tour of the building? I'd—'

'I would not.'

Tig was almost at the railing now. She stretched to grab it and as she did so, Cold Annie reached out a hand towards her.

Tig gasped as cold fingers brushed hers. She yanked her arm back and felt the toes of her left foot slip over the edge of the beam. She wobbled forward and fell onto one knee, letting go of the light-stick to save herself.

Too late, she realized her mistake. The stick performed a perfect somersault as it fell, the wooden handle hitting the top of the blanket-wrapped machine before clattering onto the boards of the stage.

'Euphonia!' cried the professor.

Snell looked directly up at Tig.

She glanced up towards Annie, as if the ghost might somehow save her, but she was gone.

There was a painfully long moment of silence as Snell drew breath, then bellowed, 'How dare you?!'

Enter Professor Faber,
Stage Right

'**G**et down at once, girl!' shouted Snell.

Shaken from her almost-fall, Tig didn't dare stand up again. She shuffled herself along the girder to the walkway and ducked under the railings before getting to her feet. Snell's furious stare followed her.

She descended the ladder into the Green Room, a hollow feeling of dread in her stomach. What if she'd broken the professor's machine? She had been so excited to meet him and she'd already ruined it. Meeting the new performers was one of the best bits of life at the Royale – they were usually warm and lively and colourful, full of stories of life on the stage. Even without this mishap, Professor Faber seemed grumpy and sharp.

Tig scurried through the room and out of the door, doubling back on herself to emerge at the side of the stage.

Professor Faber barely glanced at her, frantically untying ropes and straps. Tig took in his appearance. He was very tall – half a head bigger than Snell, and much thinner, and his clothes looked dishevelled from travel. 'What has she done to you?' he murmured to the machine.

Snell stood with his hands on his hips, nostrils flared.

'I was lighting the lamps and there was—' Tig cut herself off. Perhaps she shouldn't mention Cold Annie to Snell, particularly in front of a visitor. Snell scoffed at theatre superstitions and wouldn't take kindly to talk of ghosts. She picked up the light-stick. The fall had extinguished the flame. 'It was an accident.'

'How dare you show me up like this?' growled Snell. 'And look at the state of you! A disgrace.'

Tig glanced down. Her normally pale hands were covered in grime and a big smudge of dust covered one of her sleeves. Her faded dress was more repair than fabric. She pushed her hair back – she had started the day with a neatly tied bun but as usual, it had come loose and fell messily around her face. She felt hot, and embarrassed. This wasn't the first impression she had hoped to make on the professor.

'...extremely fragile...' Professor Faber was muttering through clenched teeth.

Snell gripped Tig's shoulder, fingers digging in, hard.

'So sorry, Mr Faber.' He bowed slightly, his tone switching from sharp to grovelling. He ran his free hand through his hair, which was too black for a man of his age, as though he had greased it with boot polish.

'Professor.'

'*Professor* Faber,' Snell corrected. 'I apologize for this unruly child. My sister, you see, is too soft-hearted. She insists on keeping all sorts of flotsam around.'

Tig clenched her jaw. Snell would say anything to make himself look good, but he was the reason the only year-round workers there were children: he was too cheap to pay adult wages.

'This is unacceptable!'

Snell bowed once more. 'It won't happen again.'

Professor Faber pulled back the covering from his creation, and Tig gasped.

She had expected something impressive – a mechanical marvel of gears and clockwork, a wind-up music box with a moving mouth – but she had never expected this. It was a *human face*.

Tig leaned in to get a closer look, and Snell did too, despite his anger. The moving-blankets fell away to reveal a perfectly realistic female face, surrounded by dark ringlets, mounted onto a metal frame. Behind the mask lay row upon row of brass levers and pincers, gleaming gold under the gaslights. Each one led down through a series of complicated corners and twists to a row of piano keys. The whole thing was mounted on an ornate table, giving the impression of a centaur – but instead of half-man, half-horse, the machine was half-woman, half-harpsichord.

'She's beautiful,' whispered Tig.

'She is *damaged*.' The professor clenched his fists, and then

13

folded his arms tightly across his chest as though to keep from lashing out.

'It doesn't look—' Snell began, but the professor gave him such a fierce stare that he stopped.

'The eyes! Look!'

The eyes were glass, startling blue, and looked so real they might blink at any moment. But the right one was cracked, an ugly spiderweb of white lines radiating out from the spot where the light-stick had struck it.

Tig was swamped with yellow-green guilt. It tasted like a mouthful of gravel. 'Professor, I'm so sorry, I didn't mean to—'

'Silence!' Snell gave her a quick shake to emphasise his point. 'Are the eyes necessary to make the machine talk?'

'Every part of the machine is necessary, sir!'

'Ah, yes, well, quite, but that is to say, if the talking mechanism is undamaged it shouldn't matter—'

'Shouldn't matter?' The professor's voice was growing louder.

Snell was getting red in the face. He wasn't used to people arguing with him. And that was the last thing the Royale needed – another person for Snell to butt heads with. It was bad enough dealing with the daily arguments between him and Eliza, his sister and co-owner of the theatre.

'Perhaps it can be fixed, professor?' said Tig, hoping to calm the situation.

'These eyes were made in Bavaria, by the best doll-makers in the world, at great expense,' said the professor.

14

'Of course, the Royale will pay for the replacement eye,' said Snell.

Tig looked up, surprised. Snell was tight-fisted and stingy – it wasn't like him to offer a farthing without great complaint. The professor's act must really be special, if the manager was willing to part with his money to keep him happy.

'Of course you will!' Professor Faber snapped back.

Snell pursed his lips. Tig could see he was trying very hard not to lose his temper, and she knew from experience he would only take it out on someone else later. Better stay well clear of him for the rest of the day.

'It will take weeks to have them made,' the professor continued. 'I expected better from this establishment.'

'Tremendously sorry, once again.' Snell made another little bow. The handkerchief was produced once more, and dabbed on his sweaty neck. 'I will ensure the person responsible—' he took hold of the back of Tig's collar, '—is suitably disciplined.'

With that he marched Tig to the back corner of the stage, behind the backdrop cloth, and roughly shoved her through the door to the workshop.

'I'll deal with you later.'

3

An Aside

The best thing to do was keep busy and avoid Mr Snell until his temper had chance to burn itself out. There was always plenty of work to do at the Royale, and most nights Tig was so tired she was asleep the moment her eyes closed. Snell was too cheap to pay set-builders and stagehands all year round, so he only hired help when a show absolutely required more workers. The only permanent staff were the three children – Gus, Tig, and Nelson, Tig's only friend.

Nelson was already working at the Royale when Tig arrived two years ago. He had been a scavenger, cleaning beneath the machinery in a cotton mill, and learned to read and write at the Ragged School on Sundays. When the teacher saw how neatly he drew his letters, and how quick he was to be helpful, she introduced him to Eliza, who hired him right away to paint the signs and the scenery.

After an hour of window-washing in the lobby, Tig found Nelson in the Minshull Gallery – a grand name for a rather disappointing little museum. It was home to half a dozen oil paintings of questionable quality, and a collection of sad-looking taxidermy animals. This was Snell's addition to the Royale. He had visited a theatre in London that had a vast exhibition room, filled with exotic stuffed animals like elephants and giraffes, and decided he wanted the same thing.

Of course, the Royale couldn't afford a stuffed giraffe; the most impressive animal in Snell's collection was a cross-eyed bear that Tig secretly thought might really be a dog. No one ever came to visit the place, but still Snell insisted it be cleaned top to bottom once a week, display cases polished, floor gleaming.

'I had to repaint the sign four times,' said Nelson, as soon as she arrived with the dustpan. He had dark skin and curly hair, and the warmest smile Tig had ever known. A rough paint-speckled apron covered his hand-me-down grey jacket. 'Snell wanted it to say "Faber's Marvellous Talking Machine" and Eliza wanted it to say "Faber's Incredible Talking Machine".'

'I'd have gone for "Faber's *Fabulous* Talking Machine",' said Tig.

'Don't you start.' Nelson rolled his eyes.

Nelson had looked out for Tig from the day she arrived at the Royale. He was from a poor family and had worked ever since he was big enough to hold a broom, but Tig's life before had been very different. Mr Rabbit had made a good living as foreman at a linen factory. There was a housekeeper and a cook, and Tig had shared a governess with another family. But when her father died – his lungs ruined from breathing the cotton fibres – Tig and her mother were left with nothing. They had ended up in a boarding house, barely scraping together the pennies for rent and food.

Now she lived at the Royale, and her mother had gone off to be governess for some other girl outside the city, though they wrote to each other as often as they could manage. The change had been difficult for Tig, all alone in the world for the very first time. Despite all the hustle and bustle and excitement of theatre life, with all its colourful secrets and fascinating visitors, she often felt sorry for herself. It felt so unfair that fate had upturned her world.

It was Nelson who'd shown her how to make the best of things. He introduced her to all the secret passageways around the building, and the places to hide when Snell was in one of his moods. He taught her how to get by on her measly wages – which food stalls could fill your belly if you only had a penny, how to use a bit of paraffin wax to stop old boots letting in water. The sort of things she'd never needed to learn before.

Nelson knew what it was like to lose someone too. His mum lay buried in a pauper's grave in Angel Meadows, and he'd been left behind with his grandmother while his dad went to find work in Liverpool shipyards.

Muffled angry voices came from the office, where Snell

and Eliza were arguing again. At least with Snell distracted, Tig could tell Nelson what she'd seen.

'I almost fell from the flies.' She knelt to hold the dustpan steady as Nelson swept. 'I dropped the light-stick and it hit the machine that's just arrived, and damaged it.'

'Ha!' Gus was leaning against a case which held a small stuffed monkey, eating an apple and not doing very much of anything. 'What an idiot.'

'Shut up, Gus,' said Tig. 'I wasn't talking to you. Anyway, I was only up there because you didn't do your job.'

'Because some of us have real work to do. You wouldn't know.' Gus was fourteen, and much more important than Tig and Nelson, at least according to him. He had disliked Tig since the first week she arrived and he had been too scared to climb into the flies to replace a broken pulley, so Tig had done it. He was teased by one of the actors for being shown up by a little girl, and ever since then he was always looking for ways to put her down.

'Heard the shouting from the other side of the building.' Gus took a big bite of his apple and continued talking with his mouth full. 'You're for it this time. Maybe he'll fire you.'

'At least I won't have to look at your ugly face every day then,' said Tig. She pointed to the door. 'Hinges need oiling. That's your job, isn't it? I can show you how, if it's too difficult.'

Gus scowled. He threw his apple core towards them and it rolled through a pile of neatly swept dirt. 'Clean that up, girl,' said Gus. 'That's your job, isn't it?' He swaggered off in the direction of the workshop.

'Horrible boy,' said Tig.

'Rotter,' agreed Nelson. He pinched his nose to mock Gus's nasal voice. 'Clean that up, girl!'

Tig glanced over her shoulder to make sure he was really gone. 'Listen. I saw her. Cold Annie. Up in the flies.'

'No!' Nelson leaned on his broom. 'Are you sure it was her? And not just a trick of the shadows?'

'She was as close to me as you are now,' said Tig.

Nelson's eyes widened.

'When she touched my hand, it was like a puddle of cold water. That's what made me lose my balance.'

'Is it true she only has one eye?'

Tig nodded.

'Were you scared?'

'Course not,' said Tig, remembering how her chest had tightened, her heart pounded. 'Surprised, is all.'

'This isn't good,' said Nelson. 'Not good at all. You know what they say about Annie. She always appears before a show goes wrong.'

Out of the corner of her eye Tig saw Gus returning, oil can in hand, so she kept her voice quiet and moved a little closer to Nelson. 'Do you believe that?'

Nelson nodded solemnly. 'I know someone at home, whose cousin used to know someone who knew her when she was alive. He said Annie always sensed when they were going to have a bad night. She had the gift.'

'I heard she knew it was her last performance,' said Tig.

'That's right,' said Nelson.

'She was playing a death scene and when it was time to stand up and take a bow, she didn't get up. She was really dead.' Tig sighed.

'I heard it was murder,' said Nelson. 'A rival opera singer put poison in her wine.'

'Oh yes, I heard that too,' said Tig. 'Only the poison didn't kill her, but she couldn't sing any more, so she died of a broken heart.'

'You're both wrong,' said Gus, loudly.

'No one asked you,' said Tig. She stood up and blew the hair out of her eyes.

'Someone stole her glass eye before the show, so she couldn't see. Walked off the edge of the stage and broke all her bones.'

'That's stupid,' said Tig. 'You can't see through a glass eye. It's made of glass.'

'And how would she break all her bones falling off the stage? It's not that high.' Nelson shook his head.

'I wouldn't expect you children to understand,' snapped Gus.

Tig was about to reply when Mr Snell walked in.

'What's all this noise? Haven't you any work to do?'

'I did tell them, Mr Snell, but they were too busy playing ghost stories. I've been doing all the work alone.'

Tig smacked her hand against the nearest display case. 'Liar!'

'Silence, Miss Rabbit!' Snell shouted. 'Shame on you for shirking your duties.'

Tig clenched her jaw. The best way to handle Snell's anger

21

was to stay quiet and let him tire himself out. His bark was worse than his bite, but it was so hard to keep her mouth closed when he was wrong and she was right.

'Come to my office.' Snell walked away. 'You've already disappointed me once today – you're in big trouble.'

Gus smirked and folded his arms. Nelson offered a small smile of sympathy.

Tig shrugged and followed Snell. What would the penalty be this time?

4

Scene Setting

There had once been a set designer at the Royale who told Tig that scenery wasn't there to just make the stage look pretty. It was a symbol, used to reflect the story of the play. Storm clouds weren't simply bad weather, they were an illustration of turmoil on the horizon.

By that logic, the office was the perfect scenery for the story of Eliza and Snell's relationship. It was a struggle for power, played out one picture frame or houseplant at a time.

Eliza's large desk sat beneath the window. Snell's even bigger desk stood in front of it, so it was the first thing anyone saw when they entered the room. Eliza had a high-backed green armchair. Snell's was even higher, with gold paint on the woodwork. When Eliza hung an oil painting of a tree, Snell put up one of a forest.

Tig waited in the middle of the room, trying to look

sorry, as Snell took his time walking around his desk. The pointy leaves of a huge palm in an oversized planter rubbed uncomfortably against her arm, but there was no space to avoid it. Snell had bought it to make a point, after he had lost the month-long battle with his sister about whether they should install the gaslights. Eliza said she thought it looked intimidating.

Tig was relieved to see Eliza in her corner now. Whenever Snell was in a foul mood, Eliza would be extra nice, just to frustrate him.

'Tig, pet, welcome,' said Eliza without looking up from her work. Even while working in the office she was dressed for a night at the opera, her whitening hair fastened up with elaborately jewelled pins and a silk scarf secured around her shoulders with a huge fabric flower. Eliza Lincoln always dressed like the star she had once been.

'Don't speak to her, Eliza, she's in disgrace.'

'Whatever you say, Edgar,' Eliza replied.

'How many times, woman? Call me Mr Snell in front of the staff!'

Eliza had defied her parents to become an actress and made her fortune in the theatre. Snell had been the dutiful son and gone into respectable business, but lost his fortune in a bad investment. He'd bet all his money on a miracle medicine which claimed to cure everything from baldness to consumption, sure to sell in the millions, but soon found out it was nothing more than horse wee and powdered chalk. When Eliza retired from acting, she bought the Royale and

24

hired her brother as the manager. Tig secretly thought that Snell was always in such a bad mood because he had never recovered from the shame of having to rely on his little sister for his income.

Snell once said that Tig reminded him of his sister, 'a woman with ideas above her station', and he had been punishing her for this ever since. At least Tig *had* ideas. Snell wouldn't know a good one if it crawled up his trouser leg and bit him on the trinkets. Hardly a week went by without Tig's meagre pay being docked for something or other, usually because she refused to keep her head down and her mouth shut.

Snell eased himself into his chair. He picked up a newspaper from his desk and slowly folded it. Tig knew he liked to keep her waiting to show he was in charge.

A letter lying on the desk caught Tig's eye and she tried to read it . . . *very interested in your property and able to pay handsomely for the . . .*

Snell noticed her looking and snatched the letter away, shoving it into his desk drawer, which he then locked. Finally, he leaned forward and laced his fingers together. 'Thanks to you, I have had a most unpleasant afternoon.'

Tig opened her mouth to respond, but Snell held up a finger to silence her.

'Mr Faber was most displeased by your shenanigans.'

'*Professor* Faber.' The words slipped out before Tig could stop herself.

'Silence!' Snell rapped the desk with his knuckles.

Eliza gave a small laugh, which she turned into a cough when Snell glared in her direction.

'He is a most disagreeable man,' he continued. 'Rude. Ungrateful. In short, I have never encountered such a difficult person. I have no doubt his month here will inflict utter misery on us all.'

Tig clasped her hands together behind her back so she wouldn't fidget. Why was Snell telling her all of this?

'You are my most troublesome employee, Miss Rabbit, and I do not think you are suited to working at the theatre. Today's mishap has only made me more convinced of that. My sister, who lacks my head for business, has persuaded me to give you one last chance.'

'A troublesome guest, and a troublesome employee,' Eliza said, and winked at Tig when Snell wasn't looking. 'If only there was a way to solve both problems at once.'

'If only,' said Snell.

'And I daresay Professor Faber will take up quite a bit of your time, Edgar. He's not used to theatre life. He's not even used to England. We'll be very busy taking care of him. It's a shame you won't be able to avoid his grumpy ways.'

'Yes, Eliza, but as you can see, I'm busy now trying to deal with Miss Rabbit and—' he stopped and stared into space for a moment. Tig could imagine a crank being turned inside his head as he realized what Eliza had said.

Eliza saw it too. She smiled and Tig and raised her eyebrows.

'*You* will be Mr Faber's assistant!' he said, with a flourish.

'What a clever idea, Edgar,' said Eliza, pretending to be

engrossed in her work. 'How ever did you think of that?'

'Really?' Tig rocked forward onto her toes. This was the best news! Disagreeable or not, being Professor Faber's assistant was an honour. To think what she could learn from a whole month with a genius inventor. Once she won him over, of course, and made up for damaging his machine. Tig tried to learn something from everyone who came through the Royale – the musicians, the designers, the actors – she absorbed every bit of theatre knowledge she possibly could. Her brain was already bubbling with ideas . . .

Snell cleared his throat, frowned, and Tig remembered that this was meant to be a punishment. She quickly rearranged her face into a look of concern and dropped her gaze to the ground.

'Oh no,' she added, quietly.

'You can be the one to deal with him. He won't take any of your nonsense, I promise you that.'

'Yes, Mr Snell.' Tig bit her lip and nodded rapidly, trying to look scared.

'A stern hand, that's what you need. He'll keep you in your place. You will obey Mr Faber at all times. You will see to it that his stay here is entirely comfortable.'

'*Professor* Faber,' Tig muttered.

'And *most* importantly, you will see to it that I never have to hear a single complaint from that man.'

'You won't, Mr Snell! I'm the perfect person for the job. I can help him with his invention, and to design the scenery, and I can show him—'

'Hush,' said Snell with a shake of the head. 'You'll be doing his cleaning, his errands, nothing more. That's all you're fit for.'

'Please, Mr Snell, I can do so much more. If you'll only give me a chance—'

'Rid yourself of these notions, girl. You're a stagehand, and a maid, and that's all you'll ever be. That's your lot in life. You can't fight your fate.'

'Yes, sir,' she said through gritted teeth. All she had to do was keep quiet until he had finished his lecture, and then she'd have her reward – the job as Faber's assistant. So what if the professor was a difficult man? Tig was used to dealing with Snell every day, and no one could be more difficult than him.

'You will report to the professor tomorrow morning. And you will continue with your regular duties around the Royale. Things have been far too easy for you, young lady.'

Easy? As if he would know. He spent half his time at the Shakespeare Inn with his friends, and hadn't done a day's hard work in his life.

'Should you displease the professor, or cause me another ounce of trouble, you will be out on your ear. Don't speak out of turn. Don't pester him with questions. Don't...' He sighed and shook his head. 'Don't be you.'

'Yes, sir.' It took all of Tig's willpower to resist jumping up and down.

Snell leaned back in his chair and opened his newspaper. 'And find some better clothes. You can't present yourself in those.' For a long minute there was no sound other than the scratch of the pen and the excited chatter inside Tig's own head. She rocked on her heels and clasped her hands together, itching to leave, but didn't dare go until Snell dismissed her. He seemed to be completely absorbed in the *Manchester Guardian*.

She cleared her throat.

Snell flicked down the corner of his paper and glared at her. 'Well? What are you still doing here?'

5

Dress Rehearsal

Tig bobbed a little curtsey and made a run for it. As she pulled open the office door, Nelson and Gus leaped back from it. They had both been listening.

'Ha!' Gus smirked as soon as the door fell closed behind her. 'You've got stuck with the mad professor. Serves you right.'

'Go stick your head in the privies, Gus.' Tig turned right and headed back through to the Minshull Gallery. Nelson walked beside her, and Gus followed along behind.

'I had to carry all his luggage in. Right moaning so-and-so, he was,' said Gus. 'So precious about his stupid machine.' He put on a bad impression of the professor's accent. 'Vatch out! Shtop! You vill hurt her!'

'He doesn't sound like that,' said Tig.

'Can't wait to see what he does when you get in trouble.

Which you will – you always do. Because you're useless.' Gus sniggered.

At the far end of the gallery, behind the stuffed bear on its hind legs, she pulled open the door to the workshop. It creaked, because of course Gus still hadn't oiled the hinges. She held it open for Nelson, then let it slam in Gus's face.

She turned to Nelson with a grin.

'I've got brilliant news! I'm going to be the professor's assistant!' She grabbed Nelson's wrist and darted across the workshop. 'Come on!'

'Where are we going?' said Nelson.

'The wardrobe.' Tig took the stairs two at a time. 'I need to find something to wear. Help me look!'

The wardrobe was at the end of a row of dressing rooms. In it were stored various bits and pieces of costumes left from twenty years or more of plays at the Royale, folded into boxes and hanging from rails.

It also happened to be Tig's bedroom. She slept behind a rack of men's suits, her thin straw mattress topped with an old fur coat and her pillowcase stuffed with some worn-out petticoats. It wasn't much, but it was cosy and private. Much better than the shared rooms in the old boarding house she'd stayed at for a while with her mother. And better than sleeping on the floor in Snell and Eliza's apartment, as she had done when she first arrived. It was nice to be near the warm kitchen stove, but Snell snored loudly enough to wake the dead, and always woke in the foulest of tempers. Up in the wardrobe she was about as far away from Snell as she could get, so it suited her just fine.

Snell hadn't wanted Tig to live at the theatre at all. It wasn't normal practice for a stagehand to live on site. Mother had sent Tig to the interview clutching a letter addressed to Mrs Eliza Lincoln, and told Tig not to read it, though of course she had opened it straight away. It said that Mother was leaving the city for work and asked Eliza to hire Tig, look out for her and let her sleep at the theatre, so she wasn't left in the boarding house alone. It had ended with 'please, do this for Antigone', which Tig always thought strange, because her mother never called her Antigone. Only her dad had ever used her full name.

Tig started rummaging through the racks for a suitable outfit.

'What are you looking for?' said Nelson, opening a box labelled 'bonnets' and peering inside.

'Anything smart.' She pulled out a black dress but the collar was ripped and it was missing two buttons.

'That's nice,' said Nelson.

'I don't have time to mend it before tomorrow.' She shoved it back into place.

'How about this?' Nelson held up a dress with a huge skirt covered in frills and ribbons. 'Imagine Snell's face if he saw you scrubbing the steps in that!'

'I can hear him already! "Miss Rabbit, you forget your place!"' She pulled out a dark blue gown and held it up to her shoulders. It trailed onto the floor.

'No good,' said Nelson. 'You'll break your neck trying to climb the ladders in that.'

'It's all too big.' She flung the dress over a bench and slumped down next to it, dejected. 'Nothing in here is going to fit me unless I grow overnight.'

'Maybe you can just cover up the dress you've got now, with a shawl or something.' He hopped up onto the other end of the bench, reaching up for some dusty boxes on the top shelf. 'There might be something in here.'

A cold draught swept through the room, rising up from Tig's toes, making the hairs on the back of her neck stand up. She looked behind her.

Cold Annie was standing in the doorway.

'Nelson?' said Tig, softly, as though Annie were a bird that might be scared away by a loud noise.

'One minute, I'm sure there was a box . . .'

'Nelson, look.' She tapped his leg and pointed.

He glanced over his shoulder and made a whimpering noise, grabbing the edge of the shelf to keep his balance.

'You see her, right?' whispered Tig.

'Uh-huh.' Nelson answered through closed lips, completely still as though a wasp had landed on him and he was scared of being stung.

The ghost made a beckoning gesture, before turning and walking down the corridor and out of sight.

'We should follow her,' said Tig, sounding braver than she felt.

'That seems like a really bad idea,' said Nelson.

Tig was already on her feet. 'Come on. She wants to help us.' Tig instinctively knew this was true. In two years at the

Royale, she'd barely glimpsed a flicker of Annie, and now she had appeared right in front of her twice in one day. It would be stupid not to follow her and find out why.

'Tig, she's ... *it's* a ghost!'

'Don't you want to know why she's suddenly showing herself?'

'Not really!' But he got down from the bench and followed close behind her as she moved out onto the corridor. They moved quietly and slowly, so as not to break the spell. The corridor was gloomy, small puddles of weak daylight spilling through the open dressing-room doors.

'Tig, what if she's dangerous?' said Nelson. 'We can't trust a ghost!'

'But you trust me, right?' said Tig.

Annie entered the room nearest the stairs, the one people said had been hers. Performers avoided it whenever they could. Those that did use it often complained of things being lost or make-up moved around.

The children followed her inside. Tig could hear the blood rushing behind her ears with every heartbeat, and she was glad that Nelson was close by. Annie crossed to the far corner, where a tall cupboard was set into the wall. It hadn't been used for a long time, so long that it was stuck shut with several layers of paint that had been applied over the years. Annie gestured towards it.

'What?' said Tig. 'What do you want?'

Annie nodded towards the cupboard.

'Should I open it?' Tig whispered to Nelson.

'No,' he said. 'But you're going to.'

Tig edged across the room, shivering as she grew closer to the spirit, and pulled at the handle. It didn't open, but she felt it give slightly, and some of the paint flaked off onto the floor.

She glanced back at Annie, who stood watching, and Nelson, who clung to the doorframe with his eyes firmly on the ghost. Tig put both hands on the cupboard handle and yanked with all her strength. It resisted for a moment and then swung fully open. A bundle of clothes, stuffed inside who knew how many years earlier, toppled out and slumped into a pile at Tig's feet.

'More clothes!' Tig laughed. 'Are you helping me find something to wear?' Perhaps she felt bad about almost making Tig fall earlier, and was trying to make up for it.

'She's gone,' said Nelson, and he was right. 'She just ... stopped being there. Oh, I don't like this at all.'

'Don't be silly,' said Tig. 'Look! I told you she wanted to help.'

She grabbed the top garment and shook it out. It was a woollen overdress in a bright, warm red. Not too fancy. Not too long or heavy. Tig stuck her arms in the sleeves and wrapped it round her. It tied with a belt around the waist.

'Nelson, what do you think?'

'Perfect,' he said, though his eyes were darting from corner to corner as though Annie might sneak up on him.

'Thank you, Annie,' she said to the empty air.

It was almost an exact fit, and much smarter than her usual brown dress. The sleeves were a bit long, but that wasn't a problem as she preferred to roll them up for working anyway.

36

The old cloudy mirror in the corner reflected a confident, put-together professor's assistant. She smoothed down the material. There were a few creases, and a slightly musty smell, but that was to be expected.

'And it has pockets!' Tig always had a hundred things to carry around – tools and chalk and string and a tinder box, ready for whatever job she might need to do next. She slipped her hands inside to see how big they were.

There was something inside the right one. Something round, cool and smooth to the touch, like a new marble. She drew it out and held it up to the light. It was white, with a nutmeg brown ring and a black spot. It wasn't a marble.

'What's that?' said Nelson.

'It's an eye.' Her heart gave an almighty thud at the realization. A one-eyed ghost had given her a coat with a glass eye in the pocket. 'It *has* to belong to Cold Annie, right?'

'Has to,' said Nelson, coming in for a closer look. Tig handed it to him. 'But why would she give it to you?'

'I don't know.' Tig was so full of sparks it was impossible to be still. She jumped up and down on the spot, squeezing her hands into tight fists. 'No – I *do* know! It's for the machine! I can fix the machine!'

Nelson stared at the eye and frowned. 'That's so strange. It's exactly the same colour as your eyes. The dark ring and everything.'

'*This* is how I'll make a good impression on the professor! I broke the eye on the talking machine but Annie gave me this one so I can fix it!'

'Perhaps you should just give the glass eye to the professor, and let him decide what to do with it,' said Nelson.

'No, I have to do it myself! I broke it, I should fix it.' Her whole body tingled with the bright blue excitement that accompanied her very best ideas. 'I'll do it tonight.'

'But Gus said the professor doesn't like people touching the machine.'

'That's why I'll do it when he's asleep. When he wakes up it'll already be fixed! It will prove to him that I'm clever and capable.' She took back the glass eye and rolled it around in her hand.

'Tig?'

'And then he'll trust me and—'

'Tig! You're going to get yourself into more trouble.'

She felt a little twinge of doubt in her plan. Nelson was the sensible one, and he was usually right. But she had such a good feeling about this. It had to be what Annie wanted her to do. 'I won't. Not this time, I'm sure of it!'

'You always say that.'

Before she could answer, the faint sound of bells from St Anne's rang out. 'Oh! It's nearly showtime!'

6

Curtain Up

It was finally time for the night's performance to begin. Tig mingled with the audience as they made their way to their seats. Nelson and Gus had got the stage ready earlier that day.

She headed up to the dress circle – the upper level of the audience. These were the cheap seats, rows of wooden benches for the poorer customers. Below them were comfortable upholstered chairs for people who could pay a little more, and on each side were private boxes for people who didn't like mixing with the riff-raff. The boxes were empty today, just as they had been for months. It had been a long time since anyone of importance had come to the Royale.

Times were hard at the theatre. Plays and operas were expensive: there were fees for the actors, singers and dancers; costumes to be made; musicians to be hired; sets to be built and painted. A handful of music halls had sprung up around Manchester and lots of people were going there instead, for songs and cheap beer. That meant less money for the Royale, and if you couldn't afford to hire the very best performers, then the most expensive seats stayed empty. Tig loved the Royale and wanted to help, but any time she had a good idea to bring in customers, she was told by Snell to 'remember her place'.

She patted her pocket, checking for the thousandth time that the glass eye was still there. The audience members were laughing and talking as they found their seats, a delicious hum of excitement moving through the rows, and shuffled and 'excuse-me'd' her way to her favourite spot, right at the front of the balcony, on the far left.

Tig peered over the railings.

Snell was there, almost directly below her. This was out of character for him, as he never bothered to watch the plays. He didn't care whether the troupes he hired were any good. It was a miracle he'd hired the professor, something new and unusual.

He was in intense conversation with a red-haired man in a brown suit. Tig was fairly sure it was Mr Albion, who owned the mill directly behind the Royale. She walked past him sometimes when she was out on errands. He liked to stand at the doors and berate his employees for not moving fast enough when they came to start their shift. Tig was so grateful that she worked here in the relative safety and comfort of the theatre, and not in that horrible man's awful factory.

Tig glanced nervously around the dress circle. It was less than half full, which was not good for opening night. And where was Nelson?

A hush fell over the waiting crowd as the heavy red curtains began to rise. Tig leaned forward over the railings. Gradually the legs of the machine came into view. Professor Faber walked onto the stage from the shadowy wings.

The machine had been dressed for the occasion – fabric was wrapped and pinned beneath the face to look like a dress. The professor, on the other hand, had not changed his suit for the show and it looked crumpled and dusty, hanging limply off his shoulders as if made for a much bigger man. Squinting at the bright footlights, he took an awkward bow and the audience offered a polite smattering of applause.

'Ladies and gentlemen,' said the professor. He cleared his throat and tried again, a little louder. '*Ladies and gentlemen*, I present Euphonia, the incredible talking machine.'

He swept one arm back towards the machine. Tig cringed a little at his stilted and uncomfortable delivery.

The acoustics in the theatre were good, but Tig was straining forward in her seat to make out his mumbled words. 'By operating a series of levers and keys, I can reproduce . . .' He coughed. 'I can, uh . . . reproduce . . . the nineteen sounds from which all spoken words are constructed.'

'He's not very good, is he?' Nelson said, suddenly appearing beside her. 'Sorry I'm late. Snell almost caught me sneaking in.'

'Why is Faber on a shipwreck?' Tig whispered back. The flats – wooden panels that stuck out from the edge of the stage – were painted to look like the broken hull of a ship with ropes and portholes. The backdrop cloth was a beach with tropical trees and jagged, seaweed-covered rocks.

'The professor said he didn't care which scenery we used, he just wanted to be left alone. So Snell said to use what was already up.'

That was typical of Snell. He loved to talk about what a great manager he was, but he didn't really care about the theatre. The poor professor looked ridiculous standing in front of the mismatched set. From up here, she could probably spit right into Snell's hair. It was tempting, but she shouldn't ...

'D'you reckon it's real, this machine, or is it just a trick?' said Nelson.

The audience were starting to whisper amongst themselves, impatient. Faber tugged on his collar and for five excruciating seconds he stood wide-eyed at the front of the stage with a look of mild panic. It seemed he had forgotten his words.

'Can't be a trick.' Tig shuffled along the bench to make room for Nelson. 'He hasn't got the showmanship to fool people.'

When it came down to it, most theatre was simply lying with style. Actors asked their audiences to forget, at least for a couple of hours, that they were sitting in a dark room in the middle of the city, and believe instead that they were in the countryside, or a royal palace, or on a storm-drenched island. Everyone knew this, and everyone was willing to play along, that was the fun of it. But to trick people, to actually make them believe their eyes when they saw the impossible, you had to gain their trust. Dazzle them, make them laugh, show a bit of confidence and swagger. Professor Faber, still frozen in the lamplight, didn't seem capable of that.

'Get on with it!' a man yelled from the stalls and there was a ripple of laughter.

Faber made a brief bow and retreated behind his machine. He sat on a stool like a pianist, and placed his fingers on the keys.

Something between a groan and a sigh came from the machine. Then the lips parted and it began to speak.

'**It is a pleasure to meet you.**' The words were slow, heavy and deep. They sounded inhuman, strange. The audience let out a collective shudder. A young man on the bench nearest Tig leaned back, disgusted.

Tig and Nelson gasped.

'**Human speech is produced by several organs of the body.**' Euphonia took a long time to pronounce each word, like a music box that was winding down. It spoke with the same Germanic accent as its creator.

The machine was really talking. It should be impossible, to make a voice come from a solid object with no brain. *It's like magic*, thought Tig. *No, better than magic*. It was the most incredible thing she had ever witnessed, and she'd already encountered Cold Annie twice that day.

'Ugh,' said Nelson, a little too loud. 'Spooky.'

The man beside Tig nodded in agreement. Only the lips moved on the machine's face; its expression remained calm and blank as it stared over the heads of the audience.

As Faber pressed the keys, the brass rods twitched and glinted.

Tig looked around at the audience. Most shared a look of horror, some were shifting uneasily in their seats. Tig's excitement was quickly replaced by dark blue disappointment. They didn't care if it was miraculous – they hated it.

'**I met the King of Bavaria**,' said the machine.

Nelson was right. Brilliant or not, the voice was creepy, and Faber himself was no performer. What on earth had made Snell choose such a disastrous act? He had seen it in London and wittered on and on about how it was the perfect show for the Royale. She risked another glance over the balcony railings, expecting to see him looking grumpy and frustrated with the professor's poor show. But, as far as she could see in the dim light, he and his friend were whispering together, and laughing. Perhaps he just had terrible taste.

Though the performance wasn't as long as a regular play, it seemed to drag on for ever. Faber rounded off the show with a rendition of 'God Save the Queen', which sounded more like a curse on Her Majesty than a blessing. Then the professor took an awkward bow before walking rapidly off stage, leaving the audience to limply applaud an empty theatre.

'I never thought I'd live to see such a thing,' said one lady to her companion as they rose to leave. 'And I hope I never see it again.'

'Ghastly,' said someone else. 'Unnatural and unpleasant. I have half a mind to demand my money back.'

'The man is a terrible bore,' said a third. 'Whoever decided to let him on stage?'

The show was clearly doomed.

After the audience had left and the theatre was empty, Nelson headed home. Tig went about her usual evening duties, alert for any unusual happenings or more ghostly visitations.

After locking the back doors, she climbed the ladder at the edge of the stage to extinguish the gas lamps. Euphonia stood solemn and silent centre stage – the professor, it seemed, had already retreated to his quarters. After their unfortunate introduction that morning, she didn't fancy knocking on the Green Room door and asking if she could come through to put out the lights, so once again, she carefully made her away across the beams above the stage. Her heart beat harder as she reached the other side, half expecting Cold Annie to be waiting for her, but she found herself completely alone.

Before she left, Tig set a small oil lamp, safely positioned on a metal tray, towards the front of the stage. It was bad luck to leave the theatre in complete darkness. A light must be left shining for the ghosts. There was some debate over whether the light was for scaring them away, or to allow them to act out their own performances in the night. Either way, luck was important in the theatre, and Tig took this task as seriously as any other.

Besides, she would need the light later, when she returned for her secret mission to replace Euphonia's broken eye.

At the front of the stage, tucked away behind the curtain, was a small doorway into a narrow passageway, eight steps long, and barely wider than Tig's shoulders. It was totally black inside, but Tig had no problem dashing through it to the doorway on the other side. The short cut emerged behind the royal boxes, onto a long corridor leading back towards the lobby.

As she pushed on the door, she heard voices. All the audience members should be long gone by now. Snell usually saw any stragglers out personally before locking the big front doors.

The voice laughed, a reedy, unpleasant laugh the colour of tapioca pudding.

It *was* Snell.

'. . . every bit as awful as you promised, Mr Snell,' said the other voice. '*Mad* professor is correct!'

Tig froze. Something told her she shouldn't walk into the middle of this conversation.

'Quite something, isn't he?' replied Snell. 'Appalling. I saw him six weeks ago on my trip to London. I knew he was the one to pick.'

What on *earth*? Snell had known the professor would be awful, and hired him anyway? Tig crouched down to look through the tiny keyhole, but she could make out nothing but the men's legs, Snell's in pinstripe and the other man's in brown trousers. It was the mill owner, again, Albion.

'How long is his run?' he asked.

'He's booked for a month, but you've seen the man, he's a

wreck. He'll last a week. Two at most.'

'Wonderful. The sooner the better. There's room for nearly two dozen looms in there, once we rip out the stage.'

Rip out the stage and replace it with weaving looms? But that meant ... was Snell trying to sell the theatre? Eliza would never allow that.

'And you're sure Mrs Lincoln won't give us any bother?' said Albion, as though he could hear Tig's thoughts.

Snell scoffed. 'I can handle my sister. She won't have any choice but to sell when this show fails. The place has been hanging on by a thread – there won't be enough money for another show. Even a woman could understand that.'

Even a woman?! Tig thumped the wooden wall in irritation.

'What was that?' said Albion.

Tig held her breath. She shouldn't have done that.

'Probably the professor doing something to his machine,' said Snell, unconcerned. 'He's quite obsessed. Anyway, let me show you the office . . .'

Their voices faded with their footsteps as they headed towards the front of the building.

So Snell had known the professor would be a terrible act, and had hired him on purpose so the Royale would lose money. The theatre was already struggling – if Faber's show failed, he'd be able to force Eliza into selling the building. And it seemed he already had a buyer lined up and ready.

Tig had to warn Eliza.

47

7

Noises Off

As soon as she was sure that Snell and Albion were out of the way, Tig emerged from the passageway and headed to the Minshull Gallery. Here, partly concealed behind a display case of stuffed game birds, was a staircase leading down to the basement apartment shared by Snell and Eliza.

At the bottom of the stairs, Tig paused to turn off the gas stopcock. They did this for safety, every night after turning out all the lamps, as it stopped the gas coming into the building at all, so protecting them from leaks or fires. Then she knocked on the apartment door.

'Come in,' came Eliza's voice from within.

The apartment was a strange but comfortable one. The main room was a kitchen and parlour, and Eliza and Snell each had a private bedroom off it. Being beneath the theatre, the ceilings were low and there were no windows, but it was comfortable and cosy.

Eliza sat at the table, counting up the night's takings by candlelight.

'Tig!' She smiled broadly on seeing her. 'How was the show?' Although Snell forbade the stagehands from watching the performances, Eliza had never minded. She understood the irresistible pull of the spectacle.

'It was...' She paused, looking for the right word. Eliza often reminded Tig that it wasn't always wise or polite to say exactly what you were thinking, even if you were asked. She said that Tig needed to learn to be tactful, and think before she spoke, if she was to get ahead in the world. *Sometimes* Tig remembered her advice. 'I was very impressed with the invention. He's a genius. But...'

'But?'

'I don't think the audience liked it very much. Professor Faber, he's ... he's not very good.'

'Oh dear.' Eliza pushed a stack of coins aside, and wrote down a number in her ledger book. 'First night nerves, most likely. I'm sure he'll do better tomorrow, after some rest and a good meal. Speaking of which—' She counted out a shilling and sixpence and slid it across the table towards Tig. 'For the professor's meals, since you'll be the one taking care of him.'

'Thank you,' said Tig, dropping the coins into her pocket. 'Mrs Lincoln ... I need to tell you something.'

'Try to make a good impression, after what happened this morning, won't you, love?'

'I will,' said Tig. 'But listen. It's about Mr Snell. I think he wants the professor to do badly.'

Eliza set down her pen and closed the book. 'Silly girl, now why would he want that?'

'Because he wants the theatre to run out of money.'

Eliza laughed. 'My dear, if there's one thing my brother loves, it's money. You don't need to worry about that.'

'I overheard him talking. He said—'

The apartment door opened and Snell entered. Tig shut her mouth fast.

'Good evening, little sister,' said Snell, unusually jolly. He paused when he saw Tig. 'Yes, girl? Can I help you?'

'I was just going, Mr Snell,' said Tig. 'Goodnight, Mrs Lincoln.' She darted for the door.

'Yes, away with you.' Snell unpinned his cravat. 'That child, Eliza, honestly, I don't know why you—'

'Edgar, not this again.'

'If anyone respected my authority around here . . .'

Their voices were already getting louder, and Tig was relieved to leave them behind.

She ran up the stairs, through the gallery and the workshop, and up again to the dressing rooms, her brain on fire with everything that had happened that day.

Snell couldn't sell the Royale, he just *couldn't*. The thought of her beloved theatre ripped apart, the beautiful backdrops and velvet curtains replaced by noisy, soulless machinery, becoming just another of Manchester's treacherous mills – it hurt her chest to imagine.

And what would become of her? And Nelson, for that matter? They'd probably end up as mill workers themselves. The mills were where most of the poor children in Manchester spent long hours tending the loud, dangerous machines. They caught sickness in the lungs from breathing in the cotton fibres day after day. They lost their hearing from the constant noise and got injured in the machines. Nelson's own mother had succumbed to a terrible cough she caught from years spinning cotton, and his uncle had lost two of his fingers in a weaving loom.

She wouldn't let it happen.

If Snell's whole plan depended on Professor Faber's show being a failure, then Tig would make sure it was a success. As his assistant, and someone who had seen all manner of performances during her time at the Royale, she could help him. Some new scenery, a decent costume, a bit of practice at talking to an audience. The machine was amazing; there was nothing else like it in the whole world. People would *love* it. Tig would make sure of that. They would start work tomorrow, and by the end of the week the show would be the best thing the Royale had ever seen.

She needed to win the professor over, and make up for causing the earlier damage to his precious creation, otherwise he'd never trust her.

Reaching into her pocket, her hand tightened around the glass eye. It was time.

8

Quick Change

Tig waited as long as her patience would allow. The professor should be fast asleep by this time – it was better that he didn't catch her in the act, or he might stop her before she had chance to prove herself.

Passing through the workshop, she filled her pockets with a few useful items – a spanner, a small pair of pliers, some glue, some wire and a small can of oil. She wasn't sure what she might need.

The world outside was fairly quiet, though the stillness of night was punctuated by the occasional beat of a horse's hooves, and the gentle, distant hum of the mill machinery running at all hours. A city as big as Manchester never really slept, but this was as close to silence as it got. Then she crept out into the backstage area, listening intently for any sound that might suggest the professor was awake. She didn't want him to see what she was doing, as he obviously wouldn't want her to touch his invention. Best he didn't find out until she had finished, then he couldn't possibly be cross.

She was out on the stage now. The oil lamp was still burning, bathing the machine in soft, warm light. Euphonia seemed to watch her enquiringly.

'Don't worry,' Tig whispered. 'I'm a friend. I'm going to repair your broken eye.'

Gently, she touched Euphonia's face. It was cool, the rubber mask surprisingly soft.

She felt around the edges of the hair, behind the ears, and found a clip on each side, holding the wig in place. She snapped them open, and lifted the curls away in one piece, setting them down carefully on the stage.

Now she could see the top and sides of Euphonia's skull, curved sheets of brass held in place by tiny rivets. Small gaps at the sides of her head revealed the workings inside, dozens of tiny wheels and cogs and springs, more complicated than the mechanism of a clock. Tig wanted to examine them more closely but that would have to wait.

The edges of the rubber face were clearly visible now. Tig tugged in several spots, trying to figure out where it might catch, or if there was any sort of pin holding it in place. Once she was satisfied there was not, she held onto the rubber above the forehead, and began to peel it down.

There was resistance, a suction between the rubber and the metal that made Tig feel a little queasy. The face was so realistic, it felt as though she were eye-to-eye with a real woman, peeling back her skin to reveal a mechanical impostor beneath. The mask pulled away from the eyes. Rubber eyelids became limp, dark holes, misshapen now there was nothing to fill them. The naked glass eyes beneath gleamed in the candlelight.

Rounding the corner of the nose, the rubber fell away in Tig's hands. Euphonia's mouth, without the lips, looked like a vice from the woodworking shop, square and sharp, and it fell open as though in surprise. Tig yanked her hand back as the rubber tongue flopped out. She shivered.

It's just a machine she told herself. *Nothing to be scared of.* She had met an actual ghost today, and yet somehow the machine was creepier in its stillness, even without a face. As she held the empty rubber mask in her hands, the features were ugly and unfamiliar without the metal skull to hold it in shape. She set it down beside the wig.

It wasn't difficult to remove the damaged eye from its socket. Tig picked at one piece of the broken glass with her fingernail and when it came loose, so did the rest, small white chips scattering onto the stage like hailstones. Nothing on earth would make all those tiny pieces fit back together into the eye socket.

Hot panic swept over her. What if the new eye didn't fit? She should have checked before she began, and now it was too late.

Hurriedly, she pulled it out of her pocket. It looked about right and she wriggled it into place until she felt a click beneath the metal eyelid. Withdrawing her hands carefully, she stepped back to look at it.

Perfect.

Well, not *quite* perfect. The old eye had been a cool blue. This was a warm brown, and the pupil was smaller. Perhaps not what the very particular professor would have chosen, but a hundred times better than the shattered glass. In fact, Tig thought the contrasting colours looked quite magical.

She folded her arms and smiled. She had done it. Easy!

Just then she heard a creak, and whipped round, staring into the darkness, but was met with only silence. She took a deep breath and steadied her nerves, carefully picking up the mask.

It had come off so easily, but Tig couldn't quite figure out how to put it back on. She tried lining up the top of the mask with the skull, but it wouldn't stretch enough to tug down over the jaw. Next she hooked the bottom of the mask over the chin and pulled upwards, but it wouldn't stay in place.

There was another creaking sound, like feet pacing on floorboards. The professor must be awake in the Green Room!

Immediately the whole catastrophe played out in Tig's head. The professor would find her here, the machine partially disassembled, and assume she was back to cause more damage. He'd wake Snell, already angry from the earlier incident, and she'd be in for it. Possibly even fired. And if she *wasn't* fired, the professor might be so angry that he packed up and left the Royale entirely. Then Snell's wish would come true, as they'd be out of money and have to close!

All this flashed through Tig's mind in half a second. She gritted her teeth and decided to try one more time to put the mask in place. If she still couldn't do it, she would drop it and run, and hope the professor thought it had fallen off on its own.

Why hadn't she listened to Nelson? She should know by now: *always* listen to Nelson.

She pulled and stretched and – relief! The mask snapped back into position. A quick glance over her shoulder told her the professor was still inside his room. She snatched up the wig and quickly clipped it back into place. There. Almost as good as new.

Tig heard the faint click of a door opening.

Trying not to make a sound, she ran as fast as she dared, retreating to the dark of the backstage before racing upstairs and along the corridor.

She had done it! The professor was going to be so impressed with her.

9

Duologue

As soon as the first light spilled through her window, Tig was up and dressed. It had been a strange unsettled night, full of dreadful dreams and frequent waking.

In her nightmares she followed ghostly figures into the open jaws of a great mechanical face, only to realize that she was a ghost too. Trapped inside a vast clockwork maze, she searched for an escape route and found herself falling, tumbling, plummeting towards the stage, then woke with a jerk, breathless and terrified. Several times she swore she heard the machine talking, down on the stage: eerie, groaning words, muffled by distance and the thick theatre walls.

Was the voice part of the dream, too? Or perhaps the restless professor couldn't sleep, and had been practising for the next show.

The next morning, with Eliza's money in her pocket, she raced out to buy the professor some breakfast. Tig wasn't sure what people ate in Austria, so she bought him the best breakfast she could think of. Two sausages, and two slices of bread and butter, all wrapped in paper, and coffee in a mug from the kitchen. She carried it very carefully back to the auditorium, headed backstage and knocked on the Green Room door.

The handle turned and the door crept open an inch.

'Yes?'

A sliver of Faber's face appeared, one eye pressed into the gap.

'Professor Faber, I'm Tig.'

'You're the girl who damaged my machine. Go away.' The door banged shut.

This was not going to be easy or pleasant. No doubt that's what Snell had been hoping when he assigned her to be Faber's assistant. But she was not about to let Snell win – the future of the Royale depended on it. The professor would simply have to forgive her.

She knocked again.

The door opened a little further, so she could see his whole face.

'I'm to be your assistant, professor. Didn't Mr Snell say?' said Tig. 'I'm Tig Rabbit.'

'Absolutely not!' He went to close the door, but Tig stuck her boot in the gap, sloshing coffee onto the floor. He glared down at her feet in disbelief.

'I'm very sorry I hurt your machine,' she said. 'Only, I tripped because Cold Annie – well, she's our ghost, you see, so I tripped—'

'I don't care.'

'But I've made it right. I fixed it! I'm good with machinery, I can help . . .'

'It was you who replaced the eye?' His brow furrowed deeply with a look of both annoyance and curiosity.

'Yes, that's right.'

'What else did you do to it? Did you touch the mechanisms inside?'

'No, nothing, professor.'

'You should not have done that!' His voice was getting louder and louder and Tig cringed, desperately hoping Snell wouldn't hear. 'I didn't give you permission to touch her,' he shouted. 'Euphonia is a valuable and fragile piece of equipment, I will not have any more clumsy—' He suddenly stopped.

Tig took this as a good sign. She removed her foot from the door jamb. 'I found the glass eye yesterday. It was like fate or something.'

'Hush.' He held up one finger. 'What did you say your name was?'

'Tig.'

'Tig what?'

'Tig, sir.' She added a little curtsey for extra politeness.

'Silly girl. What's your last name?'

'Oh. Rabbit.'

59

A flicker of recognition crossed his face. Perhaps Snell had told him about her, after all. 'I see. Come in.' He opened the door a little wider and allowed her to shuffle into the room.

'I don't shake hands,' said Faber, not that Tig had tried.

She nodded. 'Pleased to meet you.'

They stood staring at each other for a moment. Close up, Faber was quite the tragic figure. Dark circles under his deep-set eyes suggested he had not had enough rest for years, and his suit was creased and threadbare in places. She guessed he was somewhere around forty-five, with the first hints of grey showing in his untidy hair. His eyes were sharp and intelligent, but also wary and sad. He was completely different to most of the performers Tig had seen pass through the Royale.

'I brought you breakfast.' She held up the mug and the paper bundle.

'Put it over there,' said Faber, waving towards a dressing table in the corner.

'So, how may I . . . assist?' asked Tig. She needed to make herself as useful as possible, so Snell had no cause to scold her, and so she could teach Faber all the theatrical tricks he needed to know.

He glanced around the room as though searching for ideas.

The walls were lined with mismatched chairs and one battered-looking settee. The nearest table was being used as a desk, and on it sat a large notebook that was open to a page covered in detailed plans of cogs and clockwork mechanisms. Tig longed to look more closely at the drawing. Two suit jackets hung from a rail, both as worn as the one the professor

60

was wearing. A small chest and a carpet bag seemed to be all the possessions he had brought. It wasn't much for such a long journey.

'I thought you'd be older,' said the professor.

'We met yesterday,' said Tig, feeling extremely confused.

'I remember. But I didn't think you would be Rabbit. That is, I thought Miss Rabbit would be someone else . . . Never mind.'

This whole conversation was so odd, Tig didn't know what to say. And Tig always had something to say. She shoved her hands in her pockets, and tried not to fidget.

'When you replaced the eye,' he said, 'did you notice anything unusual?'

'Unusual?'

'You didn't . . . hear anything strange?' His head was angled towards the floor, but Tig could see him watching her out of the corner of his eye.

'No? Like what?'

The professor folded his arms. Tig wondered if he was always this uncomfortable and tense. 'How was the show? Did you watch?' he asked.

'Yes!' said Tig. 'Marvellous, wonderful. The cleverest thing I ever saw.'

'Um. Thank you.' He nodded very quickly and looked down, as though praise made him uneasy. 'And the audience, did they like it?'

Tig hesitated. 'I didn't talk to any of them.'

This wasn't *exactly* a lie, and it seemed kinder than

61

telling him the complaints she had overheard. His hands unclenched, but his posture still seemed tight.

'So is there anything you need?' said Tig after another uneasy lull in the conversation. 'We've never had anyone live in the Green Room before.'

'Why do you call it the "Green Room?" This colour, it is cream, yes?' He gestured at the off-white walls.

'"Green Room" is just the name of the room. It's not to do with the colour of the walls.'

'Why?'

Tig paused, not sure of the answer. 'Because it's always been called that,' she said eventually.

'Odd.'

'Have you not performed in many theatres before, professor?'

'No,' said Faber, brow furrowed. 'Mostly I've done private viewings.'

'Well, theatres can be ever such unlucky places. You can't be too careful.' Tig thought about Cold Annie and how yesterday's show had been a disaster. Perhaps it was true that the ghost only appeared before a performance went wrong. She was about to explain this when she remembered Snell's warning to mind herself and be quiet. Best not to bother the professor with talk of ghosts. 'Aren't you going to eat your food?'

He scratched his head. 'Not now. I was just going to tune up Euphonia,' he said. 'I suppose you can watch. If you behave.'

She followed him out onto the stage, still dark except for the oil lamp she had left there the night before. It must be nearly empty by now. The talking machine sat in a pool of milky light, its face staring blankly out over rows of empty seats.

'She's incredible,' Tig said. The expressionless gaze was not quite so frightening with the professor nearby. She reached forward to press a key.

'Don't touch!' said Faber, eyes wide.

Tig jumped back. 'Sorry.'

'You must never touch her again without my permission. Give me your oath.'

Tig nodded. 'I promise.'

'If anyone else had done this—' He pointed to Euphonia's new eye, looked piercingly at Tig, then shook his head.

Another strange thing to say.

'How does it work?' she said. 'I mean, how can it talk?'

'She is a musical instrument. Not unlike a . . .' A look of irritation crossed the professor's face as he struggled for the right word. 'It goes big and small, like this.' He moved his hands together and apart repeatedly. 'And there is a small piano, on the side. And buttons.'

'An accordion?' suggested Tig.

'Accordion!' He threw up his hands. 'It sounds the same in German.'

'So the bellows,' Tig pointed, careful not to get too close, 'they're like the middle part of the accordion.'

'Correct,' said Faber. He became more animated when

63

discussing the machine, beginning to move around with a frantic energy. 'They push air through a reed. All sound is made by the ... shaking of the air.'

'Vibrations,' offered Tig.

'Sound travels, *shake shake shake*, through the air in different patterns.' He wiggled his fingers.

'Sound waves,' said Tig. She had learned about sound waves from the orchestra conductor. How to make them stronger so people on the back row could hear, or deaden them to stop noises travelling from backstage.

'You are a woman of science!'

Faber sounded pleased, and Tig swelled with pride.

'In the body, our lungs are bellows,' explained the professor, 'our vocal chords are the reed, and then the lips and teeth and tongue –' he punctuated his words with exaggerated facial movements to demonstrate the movements of the mouth – 'change the shape of the sound waves to make different noises.'

Tig nodded along eagerly.

'I press these keys, and levers and valves move in Euphonia's mouth. She can make nineteen sounds. Press the keys in the right order and she can say any word in English, or German, or French. She can sing! She can laugh!' He giggled and clapped his hands together in glee and then, quick as a whip-crack, his face snapped back to its serious expression. 'You understand what I'm telling you, yes?'

'I think so,' said Tig.

'If nobody touches the bellows, it will make no sound. If

nobody presses the keys the mouth can't form the words. Do you see?' He stooped a little, staring directly into her eyes with an uncomfortable intensity.

Tig nodded again.

'An accordion cannot play by itself.'

'No, professor, of course not.'

His gaze drifted off over the empty audience. Tig glanced back over her shoulder to see if there was anyone there.

'A machine that could talk without human assistance . . . now, wouldn't that be miraculous?' He blinked hard and turned to her abruptly. 'That's all. You can leave now.'

'Oh, right,' said Tig. 'But, I wanted to help you with your show. I have these ideas, you see, and . . .'

'No need.' He waved her away.

'I actually think that—'

'I don't care what you think.' He turned his attention to the machine, polishing the wood with a soft cloth, entirely absorbed in his work.

Frustrated, Tig tugged at her hair, which was already coming loose from its bun. This might not be as easy as she'd thought. Perhaps she should give Professor Faber some time to get used to her before she tried to give him advice on his performance. Nelson would tell her not to rush into things, not to push too hard, not to get herself into trouble. But this was important. Snell was counting on Faber's show failing, and without Tig's help, it would. She couldn't waste any time and the worry made her legs restless. She hopped from one foot to the other as she tried to decide what to do.

'Do you always fidget so?' said Faber in an irritated tone.

'Yes, sorry.' She clasped her hands together in an effort to keep still. 'Professor Faber, your machine is amazing.'

'I know.'

'And I want everyone to see it. If you'll let me, I can improve your show so more people come.'

He scowled. 'You're an extremely meddlesome child.'

'I know,' Tig admitted. 'But—'

'Go away, Miss Rabbit.'

10

Front of House

Ticket sales that night were even worse than the previous one. Tig and Nelson were on usher duty, standing in the lobby and pointing people towards their seats, and by five minutes to curtain-up the place was still two-thirds empty. The big smile Nelson wore faded between customers – he was concerned too.

Tig wondered if Professor Faber would even care. She didn't understand him. Why come to the theatre if he wasn't bothered about putting on a good show? What was the point of lugging his huge, heavy, delicate machine all the way to England in the first place?

Eliza was decked out in a dark blue dress, with so many frills and bows she barely fitted inside the ticket booth, and although she painted on a smile for the patrons who were there, Tig could see she was upset. Snell looked positively jovial, pacing around the lobby in his top hat, cheerily greeting the customers. Of course he was happy – he wanted the show to fail, so he could push his sister into selling the theatre.

As they closed the doors behind the last arrivals, Nelson nudged Tig with his elbow. 'Cheer up! It's the best day of the week!'

'How can this be a good day?' she muttered.

'It's payday! Payday pie day! Did you forget?'

Every Friday when they got their wages, Tig and Nelson would visit the street sellers on Market Street for their weekly treat. Nelson would buy a meat pie, Tig a treacle tart, and they would share. It had been their tradition ever since Tig came to the Royale – a bright spot at the end of a long week.

'Of course I didn't forget,' she said, absently. But her mind was elsewhere. If the theatre closed and they both ended up in the mills, could they still meet up for pie day? They might end up on different shifts, in different jobs, at different mills. Being separated from Nelson would hurt every bit as much as losing the theatre.

'It won't take me long to count up the takings tonight.' Eliza carried the cash box towards the office.

'Excuse me, Mr Snell?' said Nelson.

'What is it, boy?'

'It's payday, sir.'

'So it is,' said Snell with a frown. 'Another week of paying through the nose for you idle creatures to live a life of luxury.'

Idle? Luxury? Furious, Tig opened her mouth to respond but

Nelson quickly stepped in front of her, holding his hand out.

'Thank you, sir,' said Nelson, as Snell counted each penny into his palm.

'And you, Miss Rabbit.'

She put her hand out and managed a terse, 'Thank you,' through gritted teeth, then exclaimed, 'Wait! This is threepence short!'

Snell smirked. 'You're lucky I'm giving you anything at all after your behaviour yesterday.'

'But you said looking after the professor was my punishment,' she protested.

'It is.' Snell put the remainder of his money back into his pocket. 'Your wages are docked for the cost of the damage you caused.'

'For how long?'

'As long as I see fit.' He straightened his cuffs and flicked an imaginary speck of dust from his lapel. 'Enough standing around, children! Back to work!'

Nelson darted off to get in position and lift the curtain. 'Meet you in the usual place, Tig! Pie day!'

Snell left through the front doors. Tig assumed that he was off to the pub as usual. Eliza and the children worked every hour they could to keep the Royale running smoothly. Snell just wore the title of 'manager' like a medal, enjoying the glory and avoiding the work.

Tig stared after him, smothered by the weight of her anger. She hated feeling so helpless. It wasn't right that he could treat them so badly and they just had to take it. It wasn't right that he was plotting to steal the theatre right out from under their feet.

She shook herself. Snell was gone. Now was her chance to tell Eliza about the conversation she had overheard between him and Mr Albion from the mill. Racing into the office, she shoved the door open so hard it banged loudly against the wall.

'Goodness me, Tig, is there a fire?'

'Mr Snell wants to sell the theatre!' She blurted out the words before the door had closed behind her.

'There's no news there, pet. He tells me once a week at least. To him, the best business is the one that brings in the largest amount of money for the smallest amount of work. He can't understand why I'd care about the art, or the stories, or the excitement. He can't count those things.' She settled into her chair and tipped out the coins from the box. 'You needn't worry. As long as I can keep the doors open, we'll be making shows here.'

But Eliza was looking very worried indeed as she sorted the coins into piles.

'He's started actually trying to sell it, though,' said Tig. 'I heard him talking to the man from the mill.'

'Mr Albion?' Eliza sighed, and straightened up a stack of half-pennies. 'He's wanted this building for years. But Edgar can't sell without me. Both of our names are on the deeds.'

'He wants the professor's show to fail, so we have no money, so you have to shut down, so he can sell the building.'

She blurted the words, rising up onto her tiptoes and shoving her hands into her pockets, unable to keep herself still.

'I'm sure the show won't fail,' said Eliza. 'It's not the first time we've had a few bad nights.'

'It can't fail! The Royale can't close! I love it here, this is my home now, and what about Nelson and—'

Eliza put her finger to her lips and Tig realized her voice had been getting louder and louder.

'You're getting yourself all worked up over nothing,' said Eliza.

'I won't let Mr Snell ruin things. He's scheming against you – I'll find a way to prove it.'

'Tig, darling, you won't help things by interfering all the time. If you're not careful, you're going to get sacked. Edgar was all set to kick you out yesterday, if I hadn't talked him round, and put the idea of you assisting Faber into his head.'

'Thank you for that,' Tig said meekly.

'You need to learn to control yourself. I can't fight your corner with Edgar for ever.' Eliza smiled gently. 'You won't go far in life unless you learn a bit of tact and to bide your time.'

'Mr Snell is no good for this place,' Tig pleaded, doing her best to sound calm. 'I wish you would send him away.'

'Edgar is the only family I have. You understand how important that is, don't you?'

This felt like a very unfair thing to say. Eliza knew that Tig was only here because her family had been split up by her father's death. She felt anger rising up again, but swallowed it down. Eliza was good to her – it wouldn't help to lose her

71

temper now. 'Well,' she said once she could trust herself not to shout, 'he would still be your brother if he didn't work here.'

'But the fact is, I need him. It's hard to do business as a woman on my own. It'd be different if my Charlie were still alive. But the banks and the printers and the tailors – they want to know there's a man of the house before they'll trade with us.'

'It's not fair,' said Tig.

'It's not,' said Eliza, sadly. 'But here we are anyway. Go on, get your work finished while Edgar is out.'

'One more thing,' said Tig. 'I saw the ghost. Cold Annie. And Nelson always says she only appears when a show is going to fail . . .'

Eliza's eyes widened and the colour drained from her face. 'But . . . that's just a superstition.'

'No, really, I saw her, close up. She only had one eye and—'

'I've got to finish counting up, Tig. I've no time for your stories tonight.'

'Nelson saw her too. Do you know who she was?' Tig continued. It was hard to let go of the thought now it was in her head, burrowing deeper and deeper into her brain.

Eliza cleared her throat. Slowly and carefully, she set down her pen on the desk. Her fingers were trembling. Tig had never seen her look nervous before. She knew something.

'You've seen her, haven't you?' Tig pressed.

'Perhaps. I . . . I'm not sure.'

'Who is she? Please tell me.' Surely Tig had a right to know who was haunting her.

'There was an accident here, a long time ago. And if there is a ghost—'

'There is.'

'*If* there is a ghost, she might be something to do with that. But the rest of it is just nonsense. Superstition, theatre talk. Don't worry yourself over it.'

'What happened to her?'

'It was very upsetting. I don't want to talk about it and you don't need to know. Can I trust you not to ask me any more questions?'

Tig nodded. Seeing Eliza upset was unpleasant. She had been angry before, but never ... frightened. She wouldn't ask Eliza any more about Cold Annie, but she was more determined than ever to find out the real story.

11

Blackout

The show was just as bad as it had been the night before. Tig couldn't bear to watch the whole thing, as the awkward silences and uncomfortable shifting of the audience made her bones ache in sympathy and embarrassment. At one point a man shouted an insult which the audience seemed to enjoy more than the show itself. Poor Professor Faber. To lift his spirits, Tig snuck out a few minutes before the end to buy him a decent supper – a hot potato, which surely nobody could object to? Her belly growled at the smell but she reminded herself that she had a good meal of her own coming very soon.

As soon as the show was over, she delivered the food to Faber, wrapped in paper, along with a knife and fork from Eliza's apartment. He didn't fully open the door, just pressed his face to the crack.

'Did you touch the food?'

'No.'

'And the seller, did they touch it with their hands?'

'No, they used tongs to lift it out of the oven.'

He stuck a hand out for the food. 'What about the fork?'

'It's from downstairs.'

'When was it washed?'

'I'm not sure...'

'Never mind. I'll wash it myself.' He closed the door, without so much as a 'thank you'.

Why were all the adults in this place such hard work?

The theatre lights were still burning – of course Gus had gone home without putting them out. Tig scaled the ladder, annoyed that she was already getting dusty marks on her new clothes. Slowly and carefully, she crossed the beam to the far side of the stage and twisted the knob to turn off the gas. The first set of lights went out. Again she cautiously edged across the beam, trying very hard not to think about how close she had come to falling last time.

'If you're there, Annie, please don't startle me until I'm back on solid ground.'

With a twist, the second set of lamps were off, and the auditorium was a cauldron of darkness.

'Idiot,' she murmured to herself. 'Should've lit the oil lamp first.' Now she'd have to climb down in the dark.

A deep groaning noise came from the stage beneath. Euphonia was speaking.

'**Follow...**' it began in its sluggish, heavy way.

Tig froze at the top of the ladder in surprise. She hadn't heard Faber emerge from his room. 'Professor?' she called.

'... the rabbit ...'

'Professor? Sorry, I didn't know you were there.' She skittered down the ladder as fast as she dared in the darkness. 'I'll bring you a lamp.'

But Faber didn't answer.

'... through the ...'

She hopped down from the third step and ran blindly back to the workshop door. 'Just a moment!' It was lucky she knew the old building well and was used to finding her way around in the dark.

'... flames.'

Flames? Surely she'd heard wrong.

The professor still hadn't responded to her and a purplish feeling of something-isn't-right settled between her shoulder blades. Why would he be playing Euphonia in the dark? Why would he ignore Tig? And why would he make it say something so strange?

As if in answer, the machine began to repeat itself.

'Follow the rabbit ...'

She found the oil lamp but fumbled with the match – her fingers were shaking and wouldn't co-operate. At last she got a spark and lit the lamp, the light bringing some relief to her fears. She put the glass globe in place over the flame and headed back out to the stage.

'... through the flames.'

76

'Here you go, professor!'

But he wasn't there. The stage was empty.

Apart from Euphonia.

12

Theatre Critics

Something strange, and maybe sinister, was going on with the professor's talking machine. Tig had heard it speaking without anyone pressing the keys — something which the professor, and her own common sense, told her was impossible.

At least, she *thought* that's what she'd heard. In the bright light of a new morning, it suddenly seemed very silly. After all, she couldn't actually see the machine while it was talking, on account of the stage being dark. So perhaps Faber had been at the controls, and stepped out of sight before she returned with the lamp.

But why? It didn't make sense for him to come out of the Green Room in the dark, to say one strange and cryptic sentence, without answering any of Tig's calls. It was the sort of thing Gus would do to scare her, but Gus wouldn't have the skills to play Euphonia, and Professor Faber didn't seem the type for pranks.

Once she'd gone downstairs to turn the gas stopcock off, she'd crept back into the theatre. She waited in the dark for what felt like hours, pulling the curtains round her shoulders for warmth, to see if the machine would speak again. But it didn't, and nor did the professor come out of his room. Eventually she was so tired she could barely stand, and had to give up and go to bed.

She wouldn't really know what she believed until she had the chance to speak to Nelson about it. He was sure to say something sensible to set her mind at rest. In any case, for now, the mystery would have to wait. There were bigger problems to deal with. They were running out of time to save the Royale, and it seemed Tig was the one to do it. She had woken that morning with a new determination. Snell was against them, Eliza wouldn't listen, and the professor was *definitely* a difficult man. But she hadn't lost the battle yet. She had to make Faber's show a success. Today she was going to convince him to let her help.

She bought him a slice of fruitcake with the last of Eliza's money, and knocked on the Green Room door. There was a moment's silence, then a scrape and a thud. 'Come in,' he said, and held the door open for her.

The table was covered with papers. A detailed diagram of Euphonia was spread out there, with inkwells and a ruler weighing down the corners to stop it from rolling up. Beside it sat a notebook with more diagrams and numbers, and writing in what must be German. The handwriting matched its creator – all sharp angles and hard edges. She nudged the book aside to make room for his breakfast, took a deep breath and launched into a persuasive speech she had been planning all morning.

'Professor, good news—'

'They hated it,' he stated, throwing the newspaper at her feet.

'Where did you get this?' said Tig.

'That man brought it. The small annoying one, with the red face.'

'Mr Snell,' said Tig.

He sank down into a chair, like a marionette whose puppeteer had dropped the strings.

She picked up the paper. It was folded to a column entitled:

'THE TALKING MACHINE'

A review. Surprising. Tig knew the reporters who usually visited the theatre, and she was certain neither of them had seen Faber's performance yet.

The article began by describing the machine. *Everyone was satisfied that there was no hoax*, it read.

'This is good,' said Tig. 'Everyone believed you.'

'He says Euphonia is Frankenstein's monster,' said the professor.

'Well,' said Tig, 'he probably means she's a human form put together from many pieces.'

'No. He means she is monstrous.'

'People *like* Frankenstein's monster,' said Tig.

'Keep going.'

She read aloud, 'The voice was so melancholy and strange, so awful, the audience could easily imagine a half-human creature, imprisoned inside the machine and forced to speak against its will.' She looked up. 'That's ... not ideal.'

'A complete failure. I should never have come to England. It was just as bad in London. Disaster.'

'But Mr Snell said...' Tig stopped herself. Snell had said the show was spectacular, and everyone loved it. Yet Faber himself admitted it went badly. Snell had booked Professor Faber precisely because he knew it would be a bad performance.

Clearly he'd been working on this plan to close the theatre for a long time.

Tig glanced at the end of the article.

'To finish, the head sang "God save the Queen", which made one think, God save the inventor.'

And God save the Royale, if we don't fix things, thought Tig.

The article wasn't wrong. Euphonia's voice did have a spooky quality to it, and Faber himself looked haunted. Nevertheless, disappointment settled over her shoulders like a shawl. This wasn't going to help matters. The success of shows relied on their reviews and this was as bad as it got.

Dropping the paper, Tig watched Faber tentatively nibble the tiniest corner of the fruitcake. She noticed the remains of the previous two meals sitting on the dressing table. The bread had been half eaten, the potato merely picked at. Both sausages lay untouched. A terrible waste.

'You didn't like the sausages?'

'I'm a . . .' He screwed up his face in concentration. 'What's the word for a person who eats no meat?'

'I've never heard of such a thing,' said Tig.

'I don't like street sellers,' he said. 'You never know if they're clean.'

'Hundreds of people eat from that stall every week. Even Nelson and me. And it's never made us sick.' She swallowed down her rising irritation. Half the workers in Manchester could only dream of such a good breakfast. Some days Tig could only stretch her wages to some bread and butter, and a pint of coffee for herself. If it wasn't for Eliza letting her make the odd bit of porridge, or drink in the apartment kitchen, Tig would be half-starved. 'You must be hungry. You haven't eaten since you got here.'

He shook his head. *What a difficult man.*

'I hope you're not coming down with something,' Tig said, trying to hide the frustration in her voice.

'Coming down with something?' said Faber. 'I don't know this expression.'

'Getting poorly,' said Tig. 'Ill. Anyway, I need to talk to you about—'

'Do you think I look ill?' Professor Faber interrupted.

'No,' said Tig but Faber was already up and looking at himself in the mirror.

'I do feel hot,' he said, putting his hand to his forehead. 'Look at my eyes, the inside of the lids.' He moved close to her and bent his knees until their eyes were level. 'What colour do you see?'

'Red?' said Tig, slightly alarmed.

'How red?'

'Um ... the usual amount of red?' said Tig. So as well as sharp-tongued, grumpy and picky, the professor was a hypochondriac.

'And the tongue?' He stuck his tongue out.

'Pink,' said Tig.

'One can't be too careful. You are not yourself sick, are you?'

'No,' said Tig, 'I'm fine.'

'No coughing, sneezing, headaches? No temperature?'

'Nothing,' said Tig, getting quite frustrated now. 'About the review—'

'The crowds, they bring all sorts of nastiness with them. My throat is sore.'

'Probably from straining your voice in the theatre,' said Tig.

'Or influenza,' he countered. 'There's a lot of it about. What are the symptoms of malaria?'

'I don't know.'

'I read about it. Big problem in swampy areas.'

'There aren't any swamps in Manchester!' Tig replied, a little too sharply. This was getting ridiculous. Faber was supposed to be a man of science – he should know better than all this nonsense.

'But there are rivers. Lots of water. That could wash it up this way.' He went back to looking down his own throat in the mirror. 'Maybe we should cancel today's performance, just in case.'

Tig felt a rising panic. The show had been advertised, some tickets had already been sold and turning people away at the door was terrible for business. Even with the bad review, *some* people would come, and they couldn't afford to miss a night's takings. If she couldn't steer him away from these thoughts, she would have to ease them instead. 'There's a chemist shop across the way. I could get you some sort of tonic, for your sore throat?'

Faber looked interested. 'Tonic. Yes, here.' He rummaged through the pocket of his threadbare jacket and produced a handful of coins. Tig was surprised. She assumed, from the way Faber dressed, that he was a man of very little means, but the coins he pressed into her hands were more money than Tig made in six weeks. Snell must be paying him extremely well. 'Throat tonic and . . . and something to ward off sickness.'

'Anything in particular?'

'Get everything you can.'

13

Supporting Cast

Tig made her way out through the workshop, hoping to find Nelson. Her mind was so crowded with thoughts, she felt it might burst open if she didn't speak to him soon. He was kneeling on the floor, painting a picture of the talking machine on a wooden board with oil paints.

'Nelson! That's brilliant.'

'Thanks.' He sat back onto his heels and looked up at her. 'But what's happened?'

'What have you heard?' Nelson couldn't possibly know about the machine talking already.

'Last night?'

'You mean with the machine?'

He raised his eyebrows and shook his head in disbelief. 'I mean you leaving me in the lurch for pie day!'

'Ohhh...' Tig pressed her fist to her forehead.

'I waited ages for you! I had to eat the pie myself. And it was cold by then.'

'I'm sorry, Nelson. I completely forgot!'

'How could you forget pie day?' He stood up, brushing sawdust from his knees.

'It was all the excitement with the professor and the machine, and then, something amazing happened. Or I think it did ... probably. You're not going to believe—'

'You're doing it again.' He pointed his paintbrush at her in an accusatory way.

'Doing what?'

'That thing you always do. As soon as you get something new and interesting to focus on you forget that anything else exists.'

'No, I don't,' she said, but her words were accompanied by the stomach-punch realization that it was true.

'Yes, you do. Remember when that magician was here and for a whole month all you wanted to talk about was how to build your own magic tricks?'

Tig folded her arms and looked down at her feet. It wasn't often Nelson got cross and she couldn't stand it. Especially since he was right.

'And you're doing it again with the talking machine. You're the professor's assistant for two days and you forget about something we've done every week for two years. You forgot about me!'

'You're right,' said Tig. 'I'm sorry. Really sorry. Does it help that I had a really good reason?'

'You always think you have a good reason.' He sighed, but he was already softening. It wasn't in his nature to stay angry for long. 'Go on, then, what is it?'

Tig grabbed his arm. 'Can't say it here. I'm going to the chemist for the professor. He's feeling a bit all-overish. Come with me.'

'I've got work to do,' he protested. 'If Snell catches me skiving...'

'We'll tell him that you...' Tig snatched the paintbrush from Nelson's fingers and threw it. It bounced off the wall and rolled beneath the workbench. 'Lost your paintbrush and needed to get another one.'

'Tig!'

'I'm sorry,' she said. 'But it's really important.'

She waited until they were across the street from the theatre. Gus had disturbingly good hearing, and she wasn't about to include him in her mystery.

'I have so much to tell you. Firstly, the talking machine can talk.'

Nelson raised one eyebrow. 'I know. That's the whole point.'

'No, I mean, I think it can *talk*. When Faber plays it, it makes the sound he tells it to, like playing the piano, right?'

'Right.' Nelson jumped up onto the doorstep of the milliner's to avoid a man pushing a dustcart.

'But last night I saw it – heard it – talking, without anyone pressing any keys. It was speaking on its own.'

'No,' said Nelson. 'You're pulling my leg.'

'Come on,' she nudged his shoulder playfully. 'I don't tell fibs, you know I don't.' Usually she was in trouble for the opposite – telling the truth when it wasn't wanted. 'When I was putting out the lights last night, Euphonia started speaking. And I was all alone!'

'Are you sure?'

'Not completely,' she admitted. 'It was dark. But I called for the professor and he didn't answer, and I'd seen him inside the Green Room not two minutes before. There was no one there. And it started talking.'

'Impossible,' said Nelson. 'It can't even open its mouth without someone pressing the right switch.'

'I know.'

'And it doesn't have a brain, so how could it even think of something to say?'

'Exactly! It's a mystery. We need to find out what's going on.'

'Hmmm…'

'You do believe me, right?' A carriage clattered past too close to the pavement and they both jumped back to avoid the splash of dirty gutter water.

'I believe that *you* believe it,' said Nelson. 'Did you ask the professor about it? Maybe there's a simple explanation.'

'Not yet,' said Tig. 'I haven't had chance because – oh, that's the other thing! Snell wants Faber's show to fail, so the theatre runs out of money.'

'He can't!'

'He wants to force Eliza to sell the building. I heard him talking to that horrible Mr Albion about it.'

'No, no, we can't lose the theatre! I don't want to go and work in Albion's mill.' She tugged Nelson's sleeve. ' If we can make the professor's show a huge success, he won't be able to do it. I've got a plan. Will you help me?'

'Course I will.'

'Good.' Tig squeezed his hand. 'Friends again?'

'Always,' said Nelson.

CHEMIST

A trip to the chemist was always a pleasant diversion. It was full of good smells and interesting packages and potions. Mr Becker, the chemist, was always experimenting with a new recipe, and the row of signs outside his shop advertised everything from fireworks to toffee, baby teething powder to Pontefract cakes.

'Wait.' Nelson checked his reflection in the window, patting the back of his curly hair and straightening his jacket. 'Ready.'

The bell over the door rang as they went inside.

'Hullo!' Matilde smiled and glided across the polished floor towards them. She was a year older than Tig, always smart and poised and ladylike. Tig was the opposite – her clothes were always smudged with oil or paint, and she was more handy with a spanner than a sewing needle. Although they were so different, Tig often thought they'd be friends, if

Mr Becker wasn't always so disapproving. Tig had to stop by once a month to pick up Snell's hair tonic and indigestion pills. If she timed her visits just right, sometimes she could talk to Matilde for ten minutes while her father was out on errands.

'Morning, Tig! And Nelson – how are you?'

Nelson made a *mmmnpf* sort of noise and nodded. Tig watched him out of the corner of her eye. This was new.

'Matilde is working,' warned Mr Becker, looking up from the boxes he was stacking on the counter. 'She has no time for idle gossip.'

'We're not here to gossip, sir,' said Tig.

'You're *always* here to gossip,' he replied. 'Haven't you got work of your own to do?'

'That's why we're here. I've been sent to buy some tonics, by my . . .' What was Faber? She supposed he was her master, since she was his assistant, though it felt more like she was his nanny. 'My boss.'

Mr Becker put down the boxes and bustled over, shooing his daughter out of the way.

'Tonics, is it? What does Mr Snell have in mind?'

'Oh, it's not Mr Snell this time, it's Professor Faber. Our performer. He's here showing his talking machine at the Royale. He has a bad throat from the exertion of the show last night.'

'Bad throat, I have the very thing. Robinson's Pastelles. Dissolve in the mouth four times a day. Or, a tonic of my own devising, based on an old remedy of my wife's family, in India.'

He moved lightly on his feet between shelves and tables, picking up a small rectangular box and slim green glass bottle. 'Which do you think your professor would prefer?'

'We'll take both,' said Tig. 'He is concerned about his health in general.'

'As we all should be!' He scurried round to the end of his counter, picked up a tiny tin and shook it, the contents rattling. 'Our patented pick-me-up pills will be just the thing for keeping a person in rude health. Good for the circulation. Promotes restful sleep.'

Tig nodded. Mr Becker was a strong salesman. He began making a neat pile of purchases on the counter.

'It's an amazing show, Mr Becker,' said Tig loudly, hoping to catch the attention of two women who were browsing the scented soaps. 'I hope you'll come. You've never seen anything like it.'

'Are you enjoying the show, Nelson?' asked Matilde, beginning to wrap their purchases in paper.

'It's, er . . . extremely superb,' said Nelson, awkwardly.

Tig did her best not to laugh. He obviously wanted to impress Matilde, and she didn't want to embarrass him. 'You should see the painting Nelson is working on, too. He's so clever.'

Matilde smiled. 'I'd like to see it.'

'It's nothing special.'

'He's just being modest,' said Tig.

As soon as Matilde stepped away to get some string Nelson elbowed Tig in the ribs and whispered, 'What are you doing?'

'I'm talking you up! You're sweet on her, I can tell.'

'Is it that obvious?'

Mr Becker was excitedly looking around the shop. 'Does he need any shaving balms? Cologne? Pomade?'

'No, I don't think so.'

'He shouldn't use that rubbish from the market. A gentleman in the public eye needs the finest grooming products.' Mr Becker was an excellent advertisement for his own products, having both a thick head of hair and a great deal of energy.

'I'll tell him, sir.'

'Master Nelson?' said Mr Becker sharply. 'Have you never seen a young lady before?'

Nelson, who had been gazing adoringly at Matilde, straightened up, mortified at being caught. 'I wasn't staring. I was looking at the shelf beside her, I think we might need . . .' He trailed off.

Matilde laughed and picked up a box from the shelf to show him. It was labelled 'Ladies' tinted lip salve – rose pink'. 'I'm not sure it's your colour.'

Tig couldn't help but giggle at Nelson's horrified expression. He put his head down as if looking for a hole in the floor he could fall into.

'Yes, yes, enough merriment,' said Mr Becker. 'Does the professor need anything else?'

'He was a little worried about . . .' Tig felt foolish saying it. 'He is worried about catching malaria.'

'In Manchester?' said Mr Becker. 'Malaria comes from

miasma off the marshes. There's no fear of malaria here.'

Tig smiled and shrugged. 'He's a cautious man.'

'Quite so,' said Mr Becker. 'I will throw in some vapour oils, with my compliments. He should smell them whenever he feels an attack of the nerves coming on.'

He tallied up the total. Four shillings and eight pence. Matilde wrapped the last of the parcels, tucking two sticks of liquorice between the layers of paper with a wink to Nelson.

'Thank you, sir,' said Tig, and they picked up the neatly wrapped parcels between them.

'Let me get the door for you,' said Matilde.

'You've got work to do, Matilde,' called Mr Becker as he retreated into his back room. 'Don't dilly-dally!'

'It was nice to see you, however briefly,' said Matilde. 'I hope to come to the theatre next week with Mama, and see the talking machine.'

'You should,' said Tig.

'It's marvellous,' added Nelson.

'Matilde!' commanded Mr Becker's voice from within.

'See you soon!' said Matilde. 'Bye, Nelson.'

'Go on, then,' said Nelson once they were a little way down the street. 'Say it.'

'Say what?' Tig stopped and rested her package on a railing to pull out the liquorice sticks. She bit into the smaller one and handed the other to Nelson.

'That I made a right spoon of myself in there. I suddenly forgot how to talk like a normal person.' He slapped his palms against his cheeks. 'What will she think of me?'

'Nooo,' said Tig. 'You were fine.'

'Honestly?'

'Honestly,' said Tig. 'You were extremely superb.'

14

Special Effects

When Tig and Nelson arrived back at the theatre, all their problems were waiting for them. As they walked across the foyer Tig's body felt heavy, the weight of her task pressing down on her.

'We've got to save this place, Nelson. How could we go on without it?'

Nelson nodded solemnly, his mouth full of the chewy black sweet. Noises echoed through the building – the muffled sound of Euphonia's voice coming from the stage. They headed through the stalls door and into the auditorium.

Faber was kneeling by the machine, adjusting one of its metal rods with a spanner. As the children walked down the aisle towards the stage, Euphonia's mouth opened and it began to speak.

'An...' The sounds were as slow and laboured as always,

somewhere between a sad song and a cry of pain. But Faber wasn't pressing the keys. No doubt about it this time.

'ti . . .'

Faber sat back on his heels, looking up at the machine's face in awe. Half a second later, he noticed Tig, who was now running in his direction, and jumped to his feet.

'go . . . ne.'

Faber slammed his hands down on the keyboard, his hands spread to press lots of keys at once. The machine's words, if there were any more, jumbled into a strained, mechanical groan.

As Tig reached the front row he eased his fingers off the keys. The machine ceased its bizarre screaming.

'It's true!' yelled Nelson, coming up beside her. 'Did it . . . but you weren't . . .'

'What did it say?' said Tig, though deep down she knew exactly what it had said, and she didn't like it at all. *Antigone*.

'Nothing.' The professor wiped his face with his sleeve, his movements twitchy like those of someone who was either very distressed or very excited. Perhaps both. 'I was just testing it. Did you get me some tonic for my throat?'

Tig edged around the orchestra pit and put her packages down on the side of the stage. She began unwrapping the paper from around the tonic, but never took her eyes off Faber. Something very mysterious was going on here. Something eerie, and real. She *had* to know what it was.

'It was talking without you playing it,' said Tig. 'We both heard it, right, Nelson?'

She looked to Nelson for confirmation, and he gave a wide-eyed nod in response.

The professor took the tonic from Tig. He stared intently at the label, mouthing the words as he read the instructions.

'Professor?' said Tig. 'How did it do that?'

Faber yanked out the stopper and drank the medicine straight from the bottle. Shakily, he lowered himself to sit on the edge of the stage.

'It can't talk on its own.' The professor sighed. 'There are bellows—'

'I know about the bellows,' pressed Tig. 'You weren't touching the bellows.'

'Tig,' said Nelson, his gentle voice speaking like her conscience. He didn't need to say anything else, as she knew what he meant; *shut up now, before you make the professor angry, before he leaves this place and takes all our hopes of saving the Royale along with him.*

But she couldn't stop herself. 'Professor. How can it make a noise without anything touching the bellows?'

'You were mistaken,' said Faber sharply, glancing back over his shoulder at the machine. But Tig *knew* they weren't mistaken, and there was something in the professor's eyes that looked almost like glee. If he was happy the machine had spoken, why was he being so secretive now?

'But it said . . . It said "Antigone".'

'No, you were mistaken.'

'I heard it. Why would it say "Antigone"?' Tig demanded. 'That's my name.'

'You what?' laughed Nelson. 'You never told me that.'

'Yes, well...' Suddenly she felt overwhelmed. Tugging at her collar, even her skin felt tight. 'No one 'cept Dad ever called me that. How could the machine know my name?'

'No, it didn't. Of course not,' said Faber, but he looked surprised by this revelation too. 'Show me what else you bought from the chemist.'

Tig unpacked the various tins and pills, and repeated what the chemist had said about each one as Faber nodded along. All the while the word 'Antigone' circled inside her brain. No one knew her as Antigone at the theatre. Even if she was mistaken about the machine talking alone – even if Faber *had* been pressing the keys – what was the chance of him using that word? Her thoughts were sea-storm purple and grey as she tried to unpick all the different feelings. There was some sort of magic in play here, and she was attracted and repulsed by it at the same time.

'Here's your change,' said Nelson, and set the coins down on the stage.

'Oh.' Faber took a throat pastille from the packet. 'Miss Rabbit. Master ... ummm.'

'Nelson.'

'Whatever you think you saw ... it's best that no one else hears about it. Do you understand?'

'Yes, sir.' Nelson nodded. 'I don't think I could tell anyone if I wanted to.'

'Good,' said Faber. 'Are we clear, Miss Rabbit?'

'But—' Tig began.

'No.' He held up one finger in warning. 'Nothing happened here. You were mistaken. If you do not agree, then you can no longer be my assistant.'

There was a long silence as Tig sized him up. She wanted desperately to understand what was happening with the machine, but if the professor wasn't going to be honest with her, the next best thing was to stay on his good side. She still needed him to trust her and accept her help, if they were going to save the theatre.

She could feel Nelson's gaze on her face, begging her not to make more trouble.

'I was mistaken,' she said at last.

The moment they stepped out of the auditorium, Tig grabbed Nelson's shoulder.

'See! I told you!'

'You were right.' He began scrambling under the workbench to retrieve the paintbrush Tig had thrown earlier. 'But I don't understand what it means. How did it know your name?'

'No idea,' said Tig. 'No one has called me that in forever.'

'Ugh. It's all dusty.' He stood up, pulling away a bit of fluff that was stuck to the bristles of his brush. 'What did the machine say last night?'

'It said . . . "follow the rabbit through the flames".'

'Flames! Tig, this is scary. Why don't you seem scared?'

'If it is magic – really magic – wouldn't that be wonderful? We'd be famous then! Everyone would want to see it. We could buy a hundred theatres with the money!'

'I don't like it, Tig.' He unstoppered a bottle marked 'Poison: not to be taken' and sloshed an inch of turpentine into an empty jar. The liquid turned sapphire blue as he swirled his brush around it. 'Even if it is magic, that doesn't mean it's good magic. It could be cursed, or, or a bad omen or something. Don't rush into anything.'

This was a good point. Tig's dad would've said curses and omens were nonsense, but two years amongst the superstitious theatre-folk had taught Tig a healthy respect for such things. A cursed machine seemed no harder to credit than a ghost appearing in the dressing rooms.

'Rabbit!' Snell's booming voice came echoing from the other side of the building. It must be time for his midday tea and he didn't like to be kept waiting.

'We'll talk later,' said Tig, heading for the door. 'I need to investigate more.'

'Promise you won't do anything stupid?'

'I will not.'

'Will not do anything stupid, or will not promise?' Nelson shouted after her. 'Tig? Which one?'

Both Snell and Eliza were downstairs in the apartment. Neither were early risers – theatre hours were long and late – so Tig was usually summoned to wait on them at around lunchtime.

'About time.' Snell spoke with his mouth full. 'I've been waiting so long I had to start my own meal.' Several dollops of damson jam were turning the white tablecloth purplish from his sloppy efforts.

'Just a light breakfast for me, please, Tig,' said Eliza.

'And me,' said Snell. 'Four eggs. Poached. More toast. And some of the boiled bacon from last night, if there's any left.'

'Yes, Mr Snell.' Tig stepped on a little wooden bench to reach the pans hanging from the wall.

'A little porridge will do me, pet.' Eliza yawned, covering her mouth with her handkerchief.

'I'll make some for Professor Faber too, if you don't mind,' said Tig, scooping the oats from the dented round tin. 'He's a bit picky about the street food.'

'That's my girl,' said Eliza. 'Always thinking of others.'

'About that, sister. Clearly Mr Faber's performance isn't working,' said Snell. 'We should dismiss him.'

Tig's ears pricked up. She stood at the stove stirring the porridge and pretending not to pay attention.

'You chose this show, Edgar,' said Eliza, spooning sugar into her teacup. 'People will come. Word will start to spread. It's always the way when you show something a bit different.' She sounded very calm and casual, but Tig knew she was seriously worried.

'Different,' scoffed Snell. He bit into a piece of toast, spraying sticky, jam-covered crumbs as he spoke. 'He's terrible – a complete disaster. We can't be paying his fees if he's not bringing in the audiences.'

Tig poked the eggs furiously. The cheek of Snell, acting like he was trying to save the Royale money when this had been his plan all along. She caught Eliza's eye and gave a meaningful eyebrow wiggle to remind her of their conversation, but if Eliza understood, she ignored it.

'And then what? We can't afford to hire a new act at short notice. Better to have poor ticket sales than none at all.'

'Precisely, we can't afford it. It's high time you listened to me and—'

Tig couldn't just stand there while Snell continued his scheming. 'He's getting better!' she said. Both adults turned to look at her. 'The professor's got some amazing ideas to improve his show. He needed to get used to the place, that's all, and now he's ready to really improve his performance.'

'We don't need your input, child,' sneered Snell.

But Eliza smiled, waving him away. 'Quite right, dear. Do you hear that, Edgar? The professor may surprise us yet.'

Snell scowled as Tig placed his plate of eggs on the table. 'You don't understand how business works, Eliza.'

'You don't understand how theatre works, Edgar.'

'I say we give him until the end of the week. If he's not bringing in a full house by then, we can't afford to keep him.'

Their voices were getting louder. Tig could sense the storm coming in and she didn't want to be caught in the middle of it. She slopped out a bowl of porridge and put it in front of Eliza, then covered the pot with a lid, and wrapped a cloth around the handle.

'We'll see, Edgar.' Eliza stood up and flounced away into her bedroom.

Snell smirked to himself, and Tig couldn't stop herself from speaking.

'I know what you're doing.' She knew she shouldn't provoke him. But Snell was a cheat and a bully, and he thought he was getting away with it. Even though her heart was beating very fast, she lifted her chin and looked him in the eye.

'I doubt that,' sneered Snell. 'You're just a little girl. You don't know anything.'

'I know you're trying to ruin everything so you can sell the theatre. You're not as clever as you think.'

'That's none of your business, child,' he hissed.

'It *is* my business. I live here, and work here.'

'Not for long, if you don't watch yourself.'

They held each other's gaze for ten long seconds. Everything was silent except the roaring inside her brain.

Snell blinked first. 'You keep forgetting your place, Miss Rabbit. You need taking down a peg or two. You'd better not put one toe out of line, or you'll regret it.'

Tig snatched up the pot and spoon and darted out of the apartment, heading upstairs to the Green Room. The professor needed to eat, and he needed to listen. That's all there was to it.

'Here.' The pot came down onto the table with more of a bang than Tig intended. Faber pushed aside the notebook he was working on, this page filled with meticulous diagrams of cogs and pulleys. She itched with curiosity to see what else he might be working on, but she was feeling grumpy and annoyed, and didn't want to ask.

'What's this?' Faber lifted the lid with his sleeve pulled over his hand and peered inside as if something might jump out.

'Porridge,' said Tig. 'I made it for you, since you don't like the street food.'

'Oh.'

'In English, we say thank you.'

Tig's insides were full of sharp feelings, and they put her in no mood for his usual rudeness. If she couldn't get him to co-operate with her plan to save the theatre, everything was lost.

He pointed at the spoon. 'Did you—'

'It's clean,' she snapped.

He took a very small mouthful and chewed it for an unreasonably long time. What was going on inside that brain? What a strange, stubborn, infuriating man.

There was magic in the machine, and he was keeping her from it, even though it very clearly had something to do with her. There was no *way* the professor could have known her name was Antigone. Whether it was a wonderful and exciting kind of magic, or a dark and sinister type, she deserved to know.

'You are angry,' he said eventually.

'No.'

'You do a poor job of hiding it,' said Faber.

'Eliza says I wear my heart on my sleeve.'

Faber frowned and leaned sideways to look at Tig's arm. She smiled at this, despite her dark mood.

'It means I let my feelings show too much,' Tig explained.

'I see. I think that I, likewise, wear my heart on my . . .'

'Sleeve.'

'Yes.'

'Professor. I want to know why the machine said my name. I *need* to know.'

Faber ate in silence, refusing to meet Tig's eyes.

Her temper was rising, but she couldn't afford to make him cross. She would have to put the question aside, for now.

'I love the theatre, professor,' she said in what she hoped was a soft and reassuring voice. 'I love the sounds and the lights and the stories and the crowds.'

He prodded the food with the spoon and said nothing.

'I have a memory – one perfect golden memory – of coming here with my parents when I was very small, and seeing all the magic for the first time. I think they must have known one of the performers, because I remember someone letting us go back stage to see how it all worked. And I fell in love and I've loved it ever since. And I don't mind working late into the night or crawling around under the stage in the dark, because this is where I belong.'

'Very nice,' muttered Faber. It was hard to tell if he was even listening, but Tig pressed on.

'Only . . . I don't mean to be rude, professor, but you don't seem to like the theatre much at all.'

He stared forlornly into his breakfast. 'Wherever I go, the audiences don't like her. They don't care about what I have achieved.'

'Well then,' she chewed thoughtfully on a fingernail, 'why do you put yourself through it? It doesn't look like you're having fun.'

'No one has ever made anything like Euphonia before. And

they've tried!' He sighed. 'I've made a scientific breakthrough. I don't expect you to understand.'

'Rude,' muttered Tig.

'The point of the theatre show was to spread the word, gain me an audience with people of learning and influence.' He pushed the porridge away.

She pushed it back towards him. 'You need to eat.'

'And in truth, Miss Rabbit, I have no other way to make a living. I spent my life building Euphonia. I know I'm not a showman but...' He trailed off.

Tig could think of a dozen professions he'd be more suited to than performing, but she kept those thoughts to herself. At least he was aware things weren't working as they were. 'May I speak freely, professor?'

'Has there been a time when you did not?'

'Euphonia is incredible. She's fantastic, spectacular, but... You're not very...' She'd just have to come out and say it. Things couldn't get any better unless someone was honest with him. 'You're boring to watch.'

'Ah.' He removed his tin of Mr Becker's patented pick-me-up pills from his pocket, and shook out a handful into his palm. He swallowed them all at once without water, grimacing as they went down. 'I do know that. I ... I spent all those years in a workshop alone. I never learned how to talk to crowds.' He seemed a little hurt, but not surprised by Tig's words.

'People want excitement. The way you explain things, well, it doesn't catch their interest.'

'But it's not about me. The machine is the thing!'

'Mr Snell says if we don't fill the audience by the end of the week, he's going to cancel your show. And then no one will get to see her.'

'Mr Snell,' he repeated, with a look of disgust.

'Let me help you fix the show. Make it flashy. If we work together, we'll get the crowds in!'

He ate another spoonful of porridge then shook his head slowly.

'Please—' A single, sob rose unexpectedly like a hiccup and she quickly turned her back to the professor in case it led to tears.

'Are you crying?'

'No!' But she was close.

'Why do you care so much?'

'Because the Royale is in trouble,' she said, without looking at him. 'If your show fails the whole place will close down. And I know I can do something about it but no one will let me!'

'Ah. I see.'

'Why not just go? You're miserable and you don't care so why are you still here?'

'I sold everything to ship Euphonia across the sea. I thought people would see her value here, in this country of industry and science. And with no investors, there's no money to travel back.'

'Then you can't afford to fail, either,' said Tig.

Faber sighed. 'Very well. You can show me your *tricks*.'

'Really?' Tig turned back towards him and smiled. 'We can start today. I'll tell Nelson.'

'Wait, Miss Rabbit.'

She paused with her hand on the door handle.

'Thank you. For the food.'

15

Technical Rehearsal

Tig, Nelson and Professor Faber met in the auditorium at two thirty. That was when Snell took his regular constitutional walk, and usually followed it up with a couple of lazy hours at the Shakespeare Inn. It was their best chance of rehearsing without his interference.

'Hello again, Professor Faber!' Nelson said brightly and held out his hand, though he looked wary.

'I don't shake hands.' Faber folded his arms.

'Are we ready to get started?' Nelson rubbed his hands together. 'What's the plan, *Antigone?*'

Tig groaned. 'I wish I'd never told you that.'

'It's a good name. You should be proud of it,' said Faber. 'It's from Greek mythology – Antigone defied the king to do the right thing. There's a play about her.'

'I'm just named after an aunty or something,' Tig muttered.

'Can we get on with it? We need to figure out two things. How to make the show better, and how to get more people in to see it.'

'Second one's easy,' said Nelson. 'We just need to chuck him a jolly.'

'I beg your pardon?' said Faber.

'Chuck a jolly ... you know! Get people on the street talking about how amazing the show is! Tell them the tickets are sold out for the next two weeks.'

'But if people think there are no tickets left, they won't come.' The professor frowned.

'If people think it's sold out, they'll be begging for tickets. Everyone wants to be seen at the best shows.'

'In fact—' said Tig, catching on and smiling broadly.

'Lord Dauncy?' said Nelson, excitedly.

'Yes!' said Tig. 'Go on. Now, for the professor.'

'What *is* all this about?' Faber looked confused and Nelson quickly hurried off. 'Who is Lord Dauncy?'

'Sit down in the audience,' said Tig. 'I'll explain while we wait for Nelson to come back.'

Lord Dauncy was a character she and Nelson had made up a year ago to help with ticket sales on another slow production. A decorated general, minor aristocrat and all-round person of high fashion and good taste, Lord Dauncy had made a few notable appearances at shows that were struggling. Using leftover costumes, they dressed up a stagehand and sat him in the royal box for everyone to see. Word would get around that people of importance were visiting the Royale, and suddenly those who were not so important wanted to be seen there too.

Euphonia suddenly made a gasping, wheezing noise, as if pulling in breath. Tig jumped.

'**The circle breaks**.' Euphonia's eerie voice echoed around the empty theatre until it seemed to come from everywhere at once.

Faber leaped to his feet.

'**The chamber falls. The widow wears red.**' The lips were moving, though the keys and bellows were still. It made Tig's whole body tense and she wanted to run and run.

Faber almost shoved Tig aside to reach the machine. He jumped up onto the stage with surprising agility but by the time he reached Euphonia it was already silent again.

'You can't deny it now,' said Tig loudly. A fluttery, tingly feeling ran down her back.

Faber's eyes were so wide she could see the whites all the way around the irises.

'How does it *do* that?' she demanded.

'I don't know.' He tugged wildly at his hair. 'I don't know! It shouldn't happen. It can't happen!' He was pacing back and forth across the stage. Then suddenly, he laughed. 'Isn't it wonderful?'

Wonderful – that's what Tig had said to Nelson that morning. But somehow the more she saw and heard, the less sure she felt. She felt as drawn to the machine as a moth circling a candle flame. And just as unsafe.

Faber seemed as surprised and confused as Tig. There was

no question of it being his doing. He had created Euphonia, but he'd obviously never expected it to do this.

They were interrupted by a knocking on the theatre doors, and a voice bellowed, 'His Lordship, Solomon Dauncy, Earl of Wythenshawe!'

'Don't say anything,' Faber urged. 'Not yet. Please.'

Nelson strutted into one of the private boxes, ten feet above where Tig stood by the orchestra pit. He was wearing a grey wig and an admiral's hat over a red-and-gold-trimmed coat, and striking a noble pose. The fabrics were cheap and had been mended many times, but from a distance, framed by the carved and painted woodwork he looked like an oil painting of his namesake.

'I thought you'd be more impressed,' called Nelson, looking from Faber's pale face to Tig's shocked one. 'What's wrong?'

'The machine spoke again,' said Tig.

'Miss Rabbit!' barked Faber.

Nelson's eyes widened in surprise and he opened his mouth to shout when there was a sudden commotion on the street outside. A great, woody crash like a falling tree, and voices shouting. They were right in the middle of the huge building, so for them to hear a disturbance outside it must be very loud indeed.

Nelson reacted first, running from the box, holding the wig in place with one hand and the oversized trousers up with the other.

'Back in a moment, professor,' said Tig, then ran up the centre aisle and into the lobby.

Gus was right behind the door. 'Oi!' he shouted as she shoved past him.

Out on Spring Gardens, directly in front of the Royale, a carriage had been overturned. One of the wheels had buckled and come loose – it lay on the paving flags a few feet from Tig and Nelson. Three men were already trying to corral the horses who were rearing up in panic, while a fourth stopped traffic behind them. The road was always busy with coaches and carriages and carts, and people were gathering round the one that had fallen. Nelson stood on the theatre steps, craning his neck to see over the crowd. There was a great deal of shouting. Mr Becker was running across the street to see if anyone was injured.

Gus emerged from the building beside her. 'What were you up to in there?'

'None of your business.'

'I heard shouting.'

'Not now, Gus!' said Tig. Even in an emergency that sly little toad was looking for an excuse to make trouble for her. No doubt he hoped to catch her misbehaving and snitch to Snell.

The carriage driver appeared unhurt, though his uniform was soiled with the mud and horsemuck covering every inch of the road. He was helping a lady climb out of the carriage. The passenger lifted her black mourning veil to dab her handkerchief at a bloody cut on her brow.

Red blood. Broken circle. A widow.

A moment of horrible understanding.

Tig spun round and ran back indoors.

'Tig?' shouted Nelson, but she didn't stop to explain.

She yanked open the auditorium doors which slammed back against the wall with great force. Faber, still standing by his machine, looked startled. Tig marched down the aisle towards the stage.

'A carriage overturned outside,' she panted. 'A wheel broke.'

'What are you saying?'

'A woman was bleeding,' Tig continued. 'A woman in a mourning veil.'

Faber sat down on the stool behind Euphonia.

Tig climbed up the steps onto the stage. 'The machine said a circle would break and a chamber would fall and a widow would wear red. The wheel, and the carriage, and the blood.'

Faber rubbed his eyes.

'The machine knew what was going to happen. Euphonia predicted the future.'

'Circle breaks...' he whispered. 'Broken wheel.'

'Did you know what it was doing?' she demanded.

'No.' He ran his hands through his hair and clutched his head as though to hold his brain in place. 'She said ... in the night she said ... but I didn't.' He laughed, and then his expression transformed into one of horror. 'But that means...'

'But you *knew* she could talk on her own.' Tig paced backwards and forwards, trying to make sense of what had just happened. The machine could predict the future. This was far stranger and more wondrous than she had imagined. And completely terrifying.

114

'It only began when I got here. That first night.'

Tig was hot, burning from the inside out as a hundred emotions flickered through her at once. 'If we'd known what she was predicting, we could have stopped it.'

'Perhaps. I don't know.'

The doors opened again and Nelson appeared, with Gus at his heels a second later.

'Gus! Out!' shouted Tig. The last thing she needed was him making trouble when they were on the cusp of figuring something out.

'You can't tell me what to do!' Gus shouted back. 'I'm allowed to be here as much as you.'

'Out!' bellowed Faber, so loud it made Tig jump. Gus slithered away, slamming the door on his way out.

'What's going on?' said Nelson, making his way down the aisle towards them.

Tig turned her attention straight back to the professor. 'Why is it happening? How does she know the future? Is she some kind of ghost? Or, or angel?' Tig had seen this thing predict the future with her own eyes, and no amount of wood and brass and rubber could do that, no matter how talented the inventor.

'I don't know.'

'The future?' Nelson looked bewildered. 'Bad omens. I knew it.'

Tig was frustrated, excited, trapped. The room didn't contain enough air.

'I heard her talking that first night. I thought I'd dreamed

115

it,' Tig admitted. 'Was she predicting the future then, too?'

'Perhaps.' His voice was very calm and even. She tried her best to match his tone. 'And if this came true, maybe that prediction will, too.'

'What was it?'

Faber folded his arms across his chest. *Stubborn old man,* Tig thought.

'And last night, she said: "Follow the rabbit through the flame." What does that mean?'

'Enough questions!' he snapped. 'I don't know. All I know is that after all these years of caring for her, she's finally talking back. That must mean something.'

16

Stage Fright

Tig sat in the front row of the stalls She should be excited about her first real chance to act as director and save Faber's show, maybe even the whole Royale. But she couldn't concentrate at all. Her eyes kept wandering to Euphonia's face, wondering when the mouth might open and another prediction come out.

They'd all agreed to put the carriage accident out of their minds, and continue the rehearsal while they still had the chance. But Tig's thoughts were all shaken up and muddled.

Faber walked onto the stage. He stood front and centre and cleared his throat. 'Ladies and gentlemen.'

'Can't hear you!' shouted Nelson from the back row.

'Ladies and gentlemen,' Faber said, louder.

'Don't clasp your hands like that,' said Tig. 'It looks like you're nervous.'

Faber put his hands down, arms hanging poker-straight by his side. It was not an improvement.

'Ladies and gentlemen,' he repeated.

'Still not loud enough!' yelled Nelson.

Faber muttered something under his breath which Tig thought might have been a German swearword. His jaw was clenched in annoyance.

'Speak from your stomach, not your throat,' said Tig. 'Or you'll strain your voice.'

'The stomach does not speak,' said Faber.

Tig had never seen someone look so uncomfortable. His machine sounded more human than he did. If Tig couldn't get him to present well when it was just her and Nelson, what chance did she have of getting him to do it in front of a full audience?

'What about a few jokes?' suggested Tig.

'I don't know any jokes,' said Faber.

'Of course you don't,' muttered Tig.

Nelson jogged down the aisle towards them. 'I do! Lumpy's always telling jokes.'

'Lumpy?' said Faber. 'Is that a name?'

'My uncle,' said Nelson.

'It's Leopold really,' explained Tig, 'but when Nelson was little he couldn't—'

'I don't care,' said Faber. 'Get on with it.'

Tig gave Nelson an apologetic shrug. Prickly, ungrateful man, being so rude when they were trying to help him.

'Ahem,' said Nelson. 'What would Neptune say if

all the seas dried up?'

Faber looked on, blankly.

'I haven't a notion!' Nelson finished.

Tig giggled.

'That is a joke?' said Faber.

'Yes,' said Nelson. 'You say "I haven't a notion", meaning, I have no idea what Neptune would say.'

'I didn't say that.'

'But you would say that. In the show,' said Tig.

'And it sounds like you said "I haven't an ocean" – as in, Neptune would say that he hasn't got an ocean any more.'

'And this is funny?' said Faber, looking doubtful.

'It's definitely not funny if you have to explain it,' Nelson said mutinously. 'Try it. Get the machine to say the first bit.'

'I don't want to do jokes,' said Faber.

'Come on,' said Tig. 'You have to do something. You agreed.'

Faber sighed, but went over to the machine and sat down. Laboriously he worked through the question key by key.

'Now you answer it,' said Tig.

'I haven't any oceans,' said Faber, his expression as blank as the machine's.

'Oh dear,' sighed Tig. 'Maybe not a joke, then. Do you know any riddles?'

'Riddle is a word-puzzle, yes?'

'That's right.' Tig brightened.

'No,' said Faber, shaking his head. 'I don't know any riddles.'

'Ugh,' said Tig in frustration. 'You're not even trying, professor. Watch how it's done. Nelson?'

Nelson drew himself up dramatically. 'What gets bigger the more you share it?' he boomed.

'I don't know,' said Tig, stroking her chin in an exaggerated way like the music-hall actors did. 'What *does* get bigger the more you share it?'

'Happiness.'

'Hmm,' said Faber. 'I like that.' He cleared his throat and puffed out his chest. 'Euphonia, tell me, what gets bigger the more that you share it?'

He pressed the keys skilfully and Euphonia replied in her flat, groaning voice, '**Happiness.**'

'Fantastic!' said Tig enthusiastically. He was finally getting into the spirit of things. 'Perhaps you could try actually looking happy, at the same time.'

The edges of Faber's lips pulled outwards, in an approximation of a smile.

'A few of those,' said Tig, 'and a bit of conversation back and forth between you and the machine, and we might have a proper show.'

'Oh, and you can take suggestions from the audience!' said Nelson. 'Ask them what words you should make the machine say!'

'Yes,' said Tig. 'Like *pineapples*.'

'Or *higgledy-piggledy*.'

'Are these more jokes?' Faber said, frowning again.

'No. They're a way for you to show off your invention. To prove you can make it say anything,' Tig told him.

'Yes,' said Faber. 'That's good. I want them to appreciate

the machine, not my wit.'

'No fear of that,' said Nelson under his breath.

'What if . . .' An idea was beginning to form in Tig's head. 'What if you invited someone up to examine the machine? Let them look underneath it, and behind the curtains and stuff, to prove there's no trick.'

'No,' said Faber, quickly. 'I don't want strangers near my machine.'

'What if it was Tig?' said Nelson.

'Perhaps . . .' Faber nodded thoughtfully.

'I'm not sure,' said Tig. 'Snell might catch me up there?'

'He won't,' said Nelson. 'He's going to a card game tonight. I know because he made me shine his shoes for it.'

'Fine,' said Tig. 'I'll do it tonight, so you can practise, professor.'

A few hours later, Tig flopped down into a seat in the front row.

She was exhausted, and more than a little nervous about going up on the stage, but the sight of Nelson – no, Lord Dauncy – sitting regally in the private box cheered her up. Already she could hear whispers from the people sitting nearby, speculating about who the rich visitor might be. The seats were still fairly empty, but if tonight went to plan news would start to spread and they'd sell more tickets tomorrow.

The curtain rose. Yes, the stage looked much better. With great effort, she and Nelson had swapped out the shipwreck flats for plainer ones which looked like the inside of a library. The beach backdrop cloth had been taken down and replaced with a plain black one. They'd even adjusted the lights to surround Euphonia with a softer glow. Tig was proud of what they'd managed to do in such a short time.

Professor Faber's performance started no better than the previous night. During his introduction, he looked directly at Tig several times. She hoped the audience couldn't tell. It would spoil their plan if people realized Faber already knew her.

His voice was still too quiet as he ran through his well-rehearsed lines about the creation of the machine, and then sat down to play.

'**My name is Euphonia**,' said the machine.

Once again the audience reacted with a mix of fascination and revulsion.

Faber stood up and placed his hand behind his ear in an exaggerated listening pose.

'What's that I hear?' he said, unconvincingly. 'You do not believe my invention can really speak?'

Other people in the front row were looking at their companions, baffled, and glancing over their shoulders. It was obvious no one had said any such thing.

'Perhaps someone would volunteer to check my claims.' He pretended to look around, shielding his eyes from the theatre lights. 'You, miss, would you be so kind as to come up on stage?'

Tig tried to look surprised and flattered when he beckoned towards her. She wasn't much of an actress, but she couldn't possibly do a worse job than Faber.

She walked up on stage, self-conscious with so many pairs of eyes watching her. It was as though she had forgotten how to move her legs normally. Nevertheless, she smiled widely, determined to make this show a success.

'Welcome, stranger, whom I have never met,' said Faber. 'Please confirm there is nobody hiding in the workings of the machine.'

Tig walked slowly around the machine, standing back from it and peering beneath the tabletop. 'There's nothing here but wood and brass,' she said in a loud, clear voice, facing the audience.

Faber pulled a face that was perhaps meant to be an easy smile, but looked more like someone had put hooks in the side of his mouth and pulled. 'And would you care to check behind the curtains?'

Tig walked from one side of the stage to the other, peering behind the red curtains as though she might find something unexpected.

What she found was Gus.

Oh no!

Gus didn't normally hang around and watch the performances – he usually scurried out through the back as soon as the curtains were up. But today he was still there, standing by the ropes, arms folded, a smug look of 'you're in trouble' on his face.

Faber, unable to see Gus from his position at the front of the stage, laughed nervously. 'Did you find anything?'

'Nothing at all,' said Tig, turning back towards Faber

and the audience and trying desperately to pretend that everything was fine.

'Place your hand in front of Euphonia's mouth,' said Faber. 'I will press on the bellows and you will feel the air flowing outwards.'

'It's as though she is breathing,' said Tig, glancing towards the audience with a look of awe.

They politely applauded.

'Can it say any word at all?' said Tig. Her eyes darted to where Gus had been standing in the wings, but from the brightly lit stage she couldn't see his face.

'Suggest one,' said Faber.

Even though they had planned for this, her mind was suddenly blank. 'Theatre Royale,' she spluttered after too long a wait.

Faber nodded and slowly Euphonia began to repeat the words. The audience clapped again.

Finally, after what felt like an excruciatingly long time, Faber told Tig to sit down and she returned to her seat. It was hard to focus on the remainder of his performance – all she could think about was Gus's gloating smirk and the inevitable trouble when Snell found out she had gone up on stage.

She remained in her seat when the show was over and the audience were making their way out. Once the theatre was empty, she and Nelson met the professor on the stage.

'How was I?' he asked.

'It was good,' said Tig. 'You were good.' Her eyes darted towards the exits, wondering if Gus or Snell would stride in at any moment. Eliza might not mind, but Snell was looking for an excuse to punish her after their confrontation.

'Were the audience happy?'

'You did a grand job, professor,' said Nelson. He sat down on the stool behind Euphonia, pulling off the wig and scratching his head all over.

'Mm-hmm.' Tig nodded. She could say that Gus was lying, or mistaken. The wings are dark, she hadn't said her name . . .

'You're not paying attention, Miss Rabbit,' said Faber. 'You said you wanted to help.'

'I do,' she said.

'**Both precious things . . .**'

All three of them stared at Euphonia. Nelson tried to jump up from the stool and knocked it over.

'**Held captive below and behind . . .**'

'**. . . and within the machines.**'

The machine fell silent. Tig stepped aside but it didn't matter now. Whatever had happened, it was finished. Faber looked furious.

'Is that another prediction?' said Tig urgently.

'Lower your voice,' said Faber. He lovingly adjusted one of Euphonia's curls. 'Whatever is happening, I need to be cautious about who knows it. I can't have people interfering with my machine while I work this out.'

'What is she trying to tell us now? *Precious things*,' said Tig. 'What could that mean? Money? Ooh, treasure! Hidden treasure in a secret place!'

'Tig,' Nelson said quietly. 'You're doing it again.'

'Silence!' said Faber suddenly. 'I heard something. Is there someone else here?'

'Hold on,' said Nelson. He jogged to the back of the stage and stuck his head through the workshop door. 'Hey! You!' he called to someone out of sight.

Tig and Faber exchanged a look of concern.

'It was Gus, I'm pretty sure,' said Nelson. 'Went running as soon as he heard me coming.'

'That sneak,' said Tig.

Faber unfastened his bow tie and stuffed it into his pocket. 'We can't discuss this here.' He walked back towards the Green Room, Tig at his heels. Nelson followed, a little more reserved.

Once they were all inside the Green Room, Nelson closed the door. The professor sat down and reached for his notebook. 'I must record every detail – the time, the words, her position on the stage . . .' He dipped his pen and began to scribble more notes. Tig couldn't tell if he was excited or scared. 'If I can only work out what's causing it . . .' He tapped the end of his pen against his teeth, thoughtfully, then resumed writing.

'Behind and beneath the machine – but there wasn't anything under the machine, or behind it, just empty stage.' Tig paced the room, back and forth.

'Unless she means *under* the stage . . . Stage machinery,' said Nelson.

'I'll bet that's it! She's saying we'll find something important down there.'

'You're getting overexcited. Predicting the future is

impossible,' said Faber. He looked like a man who had seen a ghost, though Cold Annie was nowhere to be seen.

'But she predicted the carriage accident!'

'A coincidence,' said Faber. 'She didn't mention a carriage, or an accident. Sometimes, we're so keen to make sense of things we see patterns where they don't exist.'

'We have to go and look under the stage,' replied Tig. She had a gut feeling that she was right about this, and she always trusted her gut. Euphonia was telling them something important.

'Isn't it dangerous down there?' said Faber. 'You are going to get yourself hurt.'

'Yes, Tig, it *is* dangerous,' added Nelson.

'She didn't say someone was going to get hurt! If she can see the future, she'd warn us if we were in danger!' Tig protested.

'Ridiculous,' said the professor. 'We have no idea how any of this works. Even if she *could* tell the future—'

'Which she can,' said Tig. Her frustration was growing. It was so obvious to her what was happening. Why were they both being so wary and evasive?

'We have no way of knowing what she would and wouldn't tell us. Or, or if it's always true. Or what the predictions really mean.'

'That's simple,' said Tig. 'We can find out. We can test this prediction. If we find the treasure then we know she really is predicting the future.'

'She didn't say treasure, Tig!' Nelson put himself in her path to stop her pacing. 'You're getting carried away, like you always do. You're going to get in trouble – like you always do!'

'Fine!' Tig snapped. 'She didn't say treasure. But even if it's not treasure, if we find *something*, some proof that she knows the future . . .' She grabbed Nelson's hands. 'Maybe she can tell us how to save the Royale!'

A knock sounded on the Green Room door.

The Grave Trap

'Miss Rabbit, are you in there? Come out at once!' Snell! Gus must have run to tell him about Tig's appearance on stage the moment he got back from his card game. She was in for it now.

The professor saw her panicked expression and gestured for both children to stand behind the door.

'Miss Rabbit!' The knocking became more insistent.

Once they were hidden, Faber yanked the door open. 'What is the meaning of this? You know I do not like to be disturbed.'

'Apologies. I was looking for Miss Rabbit.'

'She isn't here,' said Faber.

Tig grabbed Nelson's hand and squeezed it, hoping Snell wouldn't ask to come inside. He was waiting for an excuse to dismiss her.

'Gus saw her on the stage during your show,' Snell said.

'He was mistaken.'

'With all due respect, Mr Faber—'

'Professor.'

'If Gus says he saw her—'

'He was wrong.'

She liked to hear Faber use his scathing tone on pompous Snell, even though it would put him in a terrible mood and they'd all suffer for it later.

'We don't go in for that sort of thing, here. It's not respectable to have the cleaning girl putting herself in the public eye.'

'Understood,' said Faber, sharply.

'Miss Rabbit gets foolish notions into her head,' Snell continued. 'I wouldn't want her to take advantage of your kindness.'

'I am not burdened by an excess of kindness.'

Snell chuckled. Faber stared back silently.

'And I, um...' Snell coughed uncomfortably. Faber had that effect on people. 'And nobody saw Miss Rabbit about the building during your show.'

'Do you accuse me of lying? I sent her on an errand,' said Faber. 'She is my assistant. She was needed to assist me. Leave me now.'

Tig could only imagine the indignant expression on Snell's face as Faber slammed the door on him. She relaxed away from the wall.

'That was close,' said Nelson.

131

'Thank you,' said Tig.

'For what?'

'Getting me out of trouble.'

He shrugged and turned back to his machine. 'It would be inconvenient to train a new assistant.'

'Right.' Tig smiled.

'You can leave now,' he said. 'Forget what Euphonia said. Don't do anything foolish.'

But Tig had heard two predictions now, one of which had already come true. Of course she was going to investigate.

Back in the Minshull Gallery, sitting on the floor behind the cross-eyed bear, Tig and Nelson went over the evening again, trying to make sense of what had happened. Nelson lit a candle and Tig carefully wrote down the words Euphonia had spoken.

Follow the rabbit through the flames.

The circle breaks, the chamber falls, the widow wears red.

And then this evening's prediction:

Both precious things held captive below and behind and within the machines.

'I've got to get a look under that stage,' Tig said, grimly. 'Tonight.' She needed to know if Euphonia really could see the future. And if there was something valuable hidden down there, it could solve all their problems.

'Do I have any hope of talking you out of it?' asked Nelson.

Tig shook her head and he sighed.

'In that case, I'll come with you. Just in case.'

*

They waited until the theatre fell quiet, the doors were locked and the lights were out, then went exploring.

Nelson walked ahead with the candle as they descended the stairs into hell. That was the name of the cavity directly below the stage, so called because it was hot and dark and crowded, and a wretched place to be working during a long performance. The ceiling was low and there were a hundred things to trip over and bump into.

The stage machinery was a series of trapdoors and moving platforms, operated with chains and thick ropes and great wooden wheels like parts of a great ship. When a play required an actor to appear as if by magic, or a piece of scenery to sink out of sight, a team of four or six men would be hired to work them. It was heavy, physical work and the children weren't big enough to do it themselves.

Cautiously, Nelson and Tig tiptoed around the space, shining the candle into every dark corner, examining all the spaces behind and beneath. They had to be quiet – Eliza and Snell's apartment was down on this level too, on the other side of the storage rooms. Tig's thoughts galloped like a racehorse, trying to guess what the precious things Euphonia had predicted might be. What if they were jewels, or money? She imagined Eliza's delight as Tig presented them to her, and Snell's disappointment that the theatre had been saved.

'Maybe we're here too soon,' whispered Tig. She had no idea how Euphonia worked – maybe she was predicting something that happened far into the future. Tig was cross that she hadn't thought of this earlier.

'The grave trap is directly beneath Euphonia,' said Nelson. 'That seems the most likely spot if you're going to find anything.'

The grave trap was the biggest piece of machinery they had. When the huge wheel was turned, the platform was raised and a hatch opened on the stage. It was called the grave trap because of the size and shape of the trapdoor, just big enough to lower a coffin through.

Tig walked all around it, but saw nothing unusual. She climbed up onto the platform and peered over each edge in turn. *Both precious things.* What could they be?

'I see something.' There, beneath the corner of the platform, something shiny. The candle beam had touched on something silvery. A tingly feeling cascaded from her scalp, right through her body. She reached down, but the platform was in the way. *Something precious.* She had found it.

Leaning out over the edge of the trap, Tig uncoiled a thick hemp rope from its cleat.

'Careful, Tig,' said Nelson, sounding worried. 'I don't think you should do that.'

'Come round to the side. Hold the candle low so we can see what's there.'

If she could release the rope, the weight would drop and shift the platform slightly. It was an awkward angle – the mechanism was designed to be operated by several men. The last loop came loose and the platform jolted upwards.

She was caught. Her arms were stuck.

All the breath went from Tig's body and a wave of sickness

spread over her. She had time to think *I'm in trouble* before the pain washed over her, ice-hot and crushing.

The platform had shifted unevenly because the weights had only been released at one side. Now it was wedged at a strange angle and she was wedged with it, her forearms jammed between the guard rail and the frame.

'Tig!' Nelson was on his feet straight away.

Somehow, she didn't scream. If she screamed, Snell might hear, and she had no doubt he would fire her for interfering with the machinery. Possibly Nelson, too, and she couldn't do that to him. She gritted her teeth through the pain.

She tugged at her left arm, the wood pinching her skin. Her eyes were watering.

'Don't pull,' hissed Nelson. His face was a painting of panic, and that scared Tig more than the pain. 'Try not to twist, you'll break your arms. I'll get you out. We can do it.'

What if they were already broken? The pain was hot and cold. Tig wouldn't be the first person to lose a limb in a theatre accident.

Both precious things. Nothing was more precious that her arms.

Nelson grabbed the rope and pulled, but he was skinny and the platform was heavy – especially now that Tig was on top of it.

She took a deep breath. Panicking wouldn't help. She wiggled her hands – the right side had a little more space. She twisted from her shoulder, contorting into an uncomfortable half-crouched position, and turned her wrist backwards and forwards, backwards and forwards.

Something shifted, and it gave an inch. Another deep breath, and a pull and a scrape. One arm was free, but now the pressure on her left arm had doubled as the platform tried to rise up further.

'I can almost do it,' she hissed through her teeth. 'So close. Just a little more.'

Nelson twisted the rope around his forearm and yanked down with his full weight until he was swinging from it. It worked. She pulled her other hand free and sat trembling on the platform.

Nelson dropped the rope and the platform jolted and settled. 'Are you all right?' He sounded shaken.

'You saved me,' said Tig. 'If you hadn't been here ... if I'd been alone.'

Stupid. What a stupid thing to do! She knew how dangerous the traps could be. She wriggled her fingers and rubbed her aching arms. Somehow she hadn't broken them, but a thick red stripe was already appearing across the skin.

Euphonia *was* predicting the future. Tig had misunderstood, but it had come true all the same.

Nelson offered his hand to help her down from the platform which was now wedged at an awkward angle – somebody would have to fix it. Hopefully no one would know it was Tig who'd broken it. She held the candle close to the raised corner to see what the silvery thing was that she had endangered her life for.

A broken piece of chain. That was it. Nothing precious at all.

18

Costume Call

Tig had been waiting for ever for Faber to finish checking his temperature and swallowing his various health-promoting tonics. He was the same greyish shade as when he first arrived, so they clearly weren't doing him much good. A bit of fresh air and sunshine would do more for his health, but he wouldn't hear of going for a walk. Something about factory fumes and robbers.

The Royale was noisy today. Snell had insisted the boys make some new scenery flats ready for future shows and there was a great deal of hammering and sawing. Of course, if he had his way, there wouldn't *be* any future shows. The truth was, Snell was in a bad mood and enjoyed ordering the children around.

It was a warm day, but Tig rolled down the sleeves on her coat to cover the tender bruises on her forearms from last night's narrow escape. She wasn't in the mood to explain that.

In fact, she was determined to put it out of her mind entirely. So far nothing good had come out of Euphonia's predictions. Every time the machine spoke, Tig was distracted from her true goal of saving the Royale. Besides, if she failed to fill the seats, Snell would send Faber away within the week. Then she'd never find out the truth about Euphonia. Her investigations would have to wait. It was the sort of sensible decision Nelson would make, so Tig knew it was the right one.

'Confounded noise,' muttered Faber. He was flicking through the pages of his notebook and mumbling to himself. '. . . the bellows were still, that's the real mystery . . .'

Tig had brought him up some bread and dripping, which, to her surprise, he ate without questioning her on the cleanliness of the preparation. He must be in a good mood, so it seemed like the right time to suggest more improvements to the show.

'We need to find you a proper costume.'

'What's wrong with my clothes?'

'On stage, you want something that helps you stand out.'

'I don't have anything else. And I won't go out to a tailor.'

'There might be something in the costume room that fits.' Tig tilted her head to one side. She couldn't begin to guess what size he might be, being so tall and skinny. 'A jacket, at least. Come on.'

Faber left the room very reluctantly. 'I don't want anyone in my room while I'm gone.'

'We won't be long,' said Tig.

She led him through the backstage corridors and held open the door to the costume store.

'Someone has been sleeping in here,' said Professor Faber.

'Oh, yes,' said Tig. She hurriedly gathered up her bedding and nightclothes and shoved them into a corner. 'It's me.'

'I see.' Faber wrinkled his brow and Tig felt a flush of embarrassment at her pathetic lodgings.

'Let's try one of these.' She took down a jaunty red jacket with a fur-trimmed collar.

'No,' said Faber.

'This one?' She held up a long green cloak, embroidered with stars, which had belonged to the sorcerer in the last show.

'Certainly not.'

She ran her fingers along the rows of outfits. 'Ah. Here.' She pulled out a dark blue jacket with a subtle vine-leaf pattern all over it in a lighter blue. It wouldn't stand out the way the first two might, but it certainly looked fancier than any of Faber's plain clothes, and the shiny threads would glitter under the theatre lights.

'Hmmm.' Faber didn't seem impressed.

'Try it on,' Tig urged and he reluctantly put his arms in the sleeves.

'Well?'

'Lovely,' said Tig. 'You just need...' She stood on a stool to reach a high box of cravats and rummaged until she found a bright yellow one. 'Aha!'

She passed it down to him, but he didn't take it.

139

'What's that?'

The loose sleeves had fallen as she reached up, and he was staring at the bruises on her arms.

'Nothing.' She pulled the cuffs back down to her wrists.

'What happened? Did somebody hurt you?' The concern on his face seemed so genuine that Tig felt guilty. She had to tell the truth.

'It was an accident. Last night ... Euphonia's prediction. We went down under the stage to see if we could find what she was talking about. I got caught in the moving platform.'

'You could've broken your arms.'

'Yes,' said Tig. 'That's what she meant. Both precious things. It was true.'

'Oh dear.' Faber took the cravat and began putting it on.

It was so tempting to point out that she was right about Euphonia telling the future. But she mustn't. From now on, all her energy would go into saving the Royale.

'What do you think?' said Faber.

'Now you look like a performer, not an inventor,' said Tig.

'I *am* an inventor.'

'You need to be both. Let's go to the stage, so I can see how it looks from the audience.'

They returned to the auditorium. As Tig passed Euphonia, she began to speak.

'**On the third strike the blade slips. Splintering wood. A scream.**'

Tig froze. Her sore arms throbbed as if reminding her of what happened last time.

'Don't do anything,' the professor warned. 'We don't understand it. Let me get my notes.'

'Blades. Screaming.' A little voice inside Tig's head told her to ignore Euphonia's words for the sake of the Royale and her own safety. But she could hear her own real voice already saying urgently, 'We've got to act – something terrible is going to happen!'

'I won't allow you to endanger yourself again. Give me chance to study what's happening . . .'

'Sounds like someone is going to get hurt. And we're the only ones who know. We're the only people with a chance of stopping it!'

There was a moment's silence as the last notes of Euphonia's voice echoed and disappeared into the auditorium. Then from the workshop, the sound of hammering and sawing resumed.

'The workshop,' said Tig. 'It must be about the workshop. That's the only place with blades.' She scrabbled for her pencil and paper and quickly wrote down the exact words, before she forgot them.

'Please don't.'

Faber sank down onto the stool behind Euphonia.

'Third strike. That must be the clock.' It was beginning to make sense. She could do this. 'Three o'clock. That can't be far off. What time is it now?' She looked at Faber expectantly until he sighed and pulled out his watch.

'Five until three.'

'That hardly gives us any time . . .' Tig was pacing up and down now. 'No, actually, that's perfect. If there's going to be an accident in the workshop at three o'clock, I just need to be sure it's empty then.'

She was giddy, light-headed.

'And what if it doesn't work? Haven't you learned?' The professor gestured towards her arms.

'I have to try.' She left him behind and ran to the workshop. The familiar smell of sawdust and wood glue permeated the air.

'What do you want, Rabbit?' said Gus. 'I don't need you getting in my way.'

'Where's Nelson?'

'Down in storage, looking for brackets.'

Only Gus to worry about, then. Nelson was busy, and sausages would grow on trees before Eliza or Snell picked up a tool in the workshop.

Gus had a long piece of wood balanced across the sawhorse and was holding a large saw. This must be how he was going to hurt himself.

'Isn't it time for a tea break?' asked Tig, innocently.

'I'm busy,' said Gus. 'Mr Snell says this has to be finished by the end of the day, and until I cut the support beams, we can't do anything else.'

'Since when were you so worried about your work?'

'Since Mr Snell promised me a raise.' Poor, stupid Gus. She almost felt sorry for him. He spent so much time sucking up to Snell, but Snell didn't care about him. Gus had no idea that he'd lose his job along with the rest of them if Snell got his way.

'Right,' said Tig. 'It was Mr Snell who sent me, actually. He needs you to go down to the paint shop and pick up an order. He says it's urgent.'

'You do it, then.' He lined the saw up on the wood and took a first, cautious stroke backwards.

Curse his stubbornness. 'Mr Snell wants *you* to go.'

'Why?'

'Because,' Tig forced a smile, hating her words before she spoke them, 'he thinks I'll mess it up.'

She had Gus's attention now. As much as she disliked him – and she really, really did – she couldn't bear the thought of him getting injured. He needed to work just as much as the rest of them did.

'That's true,' said Gus. 'You mess everything up. Fine.' He set down the saw. 'Where's the money?'

'What money?'

'For the order. Carter's doesn't let us pay on account.'

'Of course,' said Tig. 'I forgot.'

She took out the coins she had in her apron pocket – her meagre wages – and hesitated for a moment before handing them over to Gus.

'Course you did,' said Gus. 'Like I said. Useless.'

Tig bristled at this, but kept control of herself. She forced a polite laugh. 'That's me,' she said. 'Silly old me.'

She hopped back and held the door open for him as he strode out without a backward glance. As soon as he was out of sight, she skipped back to Faber. He had moved into the Green Room, where he was lying flat on his back on the chaise, staring blankly at the ceiling.

'I did it!'

'Is that so?' said Faber, without looking at her.

'I got Gus to put down the saw and leave the building. He won't be here when the clock strikes three, so he won't be hurt.'

'You didn't tell him, did you? You didn't tell him that the machine could talk?'

'I didn't.' Tig was frustrated. 'I thought you'd be happy! We saved someone!' She smiled, full of the warm feeling of success.

'I wouldn't celebrate yet. The clock hasn't struck.'

As if in answer, the muffled bells of St Anne's began striking the melody. Tig gestured into the air at the sound.

The clock struck. One. Two. Three—

A scream.

19

Melodrama

Tig was out of the door in an instant, and back in the carpentry workshop. Nelson was standing where Gus had been a minute before. *Impossible!* He was clutching his hand, dark red blood running in rivers down his wrist.

'Are you all right?' said Tig running over to him.

'No!'

She took him by the wrist and caught a glimpse of the cut across the back of his hand. It was wide, but fortunately didn't look deep. She pulled a clean handkerchief out of her apron pocket.

'Press this against the wound,' said Tig. She pulled over a stool and helped him to sit down.

Faber's grey face appeared at the doorway. He turned as white as a sheet at the sight of the blood then hastily retreated.

'What happened?' said Tig.

'The saw hit a knot in the wood and jumped. Ouch.'

'Why were you sawing?' said Tig.

'I was waiting for Gus to bring the next length of wood. And I came up to see what was taking so long—' He winced as Tig wrapped the handkerchief a little tighter to slow the bleeding. 'But that layabout wasn't even here. So I had to finish it myself.'

Tig felt sick. She had saved Gus, only to injure Nelson. It was all her fault! What if she hadn't interfered at all? Maybe Gus wouldn't have been hurt. Maybe he'd have finished cutting the wood before the stroke of three. Had her attempts to avoid Euphonia's prediction actually caused it to come true?

'Mind out, mind out,' Eliza called as she bustled into the room from the direction of the gallery. 'Let's have a look at it, lad.'

Tig backed away, out of the room and into the wings. Faber was polishing Euphonia, but it was clear that he was waiting for her.

'Say it, then,' she said.

'Pardon?'

'Say it. You told me so.'

'Sit down,' said Faber. 'You've had a shock.'

'Did I cause that?' She perched on the stool behind the machine. 'I tried to stop it, but I caused it to happen, right? Did I make it happen to Nelson, instead of Gus?'

Faber shrugged. 'I don't know.'

146

She couldn't stop thinking about the gash in Nelson's hand and his pinched, shocked face. Would he have to stay off work? What would happen if he got an infection? People died of such things. Tig felt the prickle of tears in the corners of her eyes.

Faber patted her shoulder awkwardly. 'There, there.'

Tig glared at him. 'There's no doubt now. Euphonia is predicting the future.'

Faber took the tin of pills from his pocket and swallowed a handful. 'I feel hot,' he said absently. 'I hope it isn't the start of a fever.'

'Oh no,' said Tig. 'You can't change the subject. She's warning us for a reason, so we can help people.'

'Who says she is warning us? She's not human. She doesn't think and feel like we do. She perhaps doesn't even know we're here.' He rubbed his forehead. 'It's like spotting shapes in the clouds. The clouds aren't doing it on purpose and they're not aware that we're watching and looking for meaning.'

'But the things Euphonia says actually happen. It'd be like spotting an elephant in the clouds and then being trampled by one.'

'I can't explain it,' he said. 'I don't know any more than you do.'

'You built her. You must know something.'

'No,' said Faber. 'I told you. It happened for the first time the night I arrived.'

'What did she say that time? Did it come true?'

He hesitated, then said reluctantly. 'She told me that I could trust you, Miss Rabbit. And whether that's true remains to be seen.'

Tig stared at the professor. Was he telling the truth, or did he know more than he was saying? He seemed pleased the machine was talking, so maybe it *had* all started when he arrived. What was it about coming to the Royale that had made Euphonia speak on her own? But Faber seemed so certain that they couldn't do anything about the predictions, it was as if he'd known about them all along.

'I think I need to lie down,' he said. 'Good day, Antigone.'

Paper the Stalls

Faber had shut himself away in the Green Room, Eliza was taking Nelson home, and Gus was still out on this errand.

Poor Nelson. Hurt because of Tig. It wasn't fair. Three people hurt in three days, all predicted by Euphonia.

Tig had tried to do the right thing, and all it had done was injure her best friend and cost her all her wages.

She should go to him, and make sure he was all right, but guilt held her back. Tig had done exactly what he begged her not to do – and what she always did. Something exciting and new had come along and she'd become obsessed, neglecting their friendship. Even when Nelson warned her to be cautious, she decided she knew better, and got them in trouble.

Sitting still with these thoughts was torture; she had to be moving. Mulling things over, she went out into the alley that ran between the back of the theatre and the mill behind. She filled a bucket from the water pump, and grated in some soap. Work would give her a welcome distraction while she tried to figure things out.

When she'd hurt her arms in the grave trap, well, maybe she deserved it. But now she'd hurt Nelson with her impulsiveness and she didn't know if she could look him in the eye. Nelson's family didn't have money to spare – if he was too hurt to work, they'd be in trouble. His grandma and uncle had always been kind to Tig, and she couldn't bear to see them suffer.

His family would be in trouble if the theatre closed, too. Tig couldn't un-injure his hand, but she could keep fighting for the Royale. Faber's act was improving but that would make no difference unless more people started buying tickets. Waiting for word to spread naturally would take too long. She needed to get people through the door, and quickly.

She carried the bucket and scrubbing brush to the lobby and climbed the stairs to start cleaning the tiles up on the balcony.

Barely two minutes later, the front door opened and in came a small man wearing a brown coat and fawn top hat.

'Good afternoon,' he called. 'I'd like to buy some tickets, please.'

Tig put down her scrubbing brush and wiped her hands on her apron, ready to go to his aid, but before she got to her feet, Snell had emerged from the office.

'We open at six thirty, my good man,' Snell said.

'Ah, yes.' The man touched the brim of his hat politely. 'I'm actually looking to purchase a large number of tickets, for the boys at the music school. Fifty-four, altogether, in the stalls. I thought I'd better come down early, make sure you can fit us all in.'

Tig poked her head over the balcony. Fantastic! The seats in the stalls were worth more than those in the dress circle, at fourpence a piece. This would be a big help.

'No, I'm sorry. We can't accommodate you.'

What? Snell was turning away badly-needed sales. If anyone needed proof that Snell was trying to sabotage the theatre, this was it!

'Oh,' said the man. 'Are you sure? It doesn't have to be tonight, if you're too full.'

'Completely sold out, I'm afraid.'

'For the whole month?'

'Tremendously sorry you've wasted your time, sir. I won't keep you a moment longer.' Snell began ushering the dismayed-looking man towards the door.

'Oh, I see. Well, thank you for your time. Good day, then.'

'Good day!'

The man left, and Snell returned to his office.

Tig wasn't about to let this happen. She came down the stairs as fast as she dared, not wanting her shoes to make too much noise on the marble steps. She opened the ticket booth, and helped herself to a roll of tickets, and after a quick glance over her shoulder to make sure Snell wasn't watching, she ran out after the man from the music school.

'Excuse me!' she shouted, dodging between people walking. The street was noisy with the clatter of hoofbeats and voices of the street sellers, and it was beginning to rain. 'Sir! Excuse me!'

She caught up to him on the street corner, and he looked most surprised.

'I'm from the Theatre Royale,' said Tig. 'We made a mistake, I'm sorry! We can sell you tickets for tonight.' She waved the roll of tickets at him, slightly breathless.

'Oh, well, that is good news.' He reached into his pocket. 'How much for fifty-four?'

'Umm...' Tig counted it out in her head. 'Three tickets for a shilling ... eighteen shillings, please.'

He handed her a pound note. 'Keep the change. The lads will be thrilled. We were going to take them to the opera for this month's outing, but they begged to come here instead.'

Twenty-two, twenty-four, twenty-six... She unwrapped the tickets from the roll, folding them back and forth into a neat stack.

'We all read the review in the *Guardian*. Sounded ghastly to me!' the man said in a jolly voice. 'No offence intended. That's why the boys are so keen to see it, I suspect. You know what boys are like, with their ghost stories and their dreadful comics.'

'Fifty-four.' Tig tore off the strip of pink tickets and handed them over. 'Thank you, sir. I'm sure your boys will enjoy themselves.'

'No doubt they will.' He tucked the tickets safely into his pocket. 'Good day to you, miss.'

Of course . . .

The newspaper article said it was creepy, and half the audience seemed to agree.

Maybe that was it. Maybe the Royale was coming at this from the wrong angle. They had advertised Euphonia as a miracle of science, a mechanical marvel, and a wondrous achievement. And people were disappointed.

But what if they advertised her as a bizarre and morbid spectacle? People flocked to see spooky stories – *Frankenstein* and *Hamlet* and phantasmagoria. When the circus came to town, everyone wanted to see the freak shows and the fortune-tellers.

The streets were getting busy. It was almost time for shift-change at the cotton mill. Men and women and children were beginning to make their way to their workspaces and soon others would be on their way home.

Tig counted the tickets in her hand. Forty-six left on the roll. If they could get a full house, just once, if people heard that the machine was so strange and hideous and disturbing that the whole theatre was sold out . . .

She crossed the road to where a group of factory workers were queuing for bread and coffee. ''Scuse me,' she said to the smallest one, a lad of about ten. 'Would you like a ticket to tonight's show at the Theatre Royale?'

'Dunno,' said the boy. 'What is it?'

'It's a scary machine that can talk with a human voice,'

said Tig. 'It was invented by a mad professor. It's got a woman's face and it sounds like it's talking from the depths of hell.' She ripped a ticket off the roll. 'You've never seen anything like it.'

'How much?' said the lad. Another boy, behind him, was paying attention too.

'Free,' said Tig. 'Tonight only.' She held out the ticket and when he went to take it, pulled it back. 'On one condition.'

'Go on?'

'You tell everyone that you're going. And tell them that's it's sold out.'

'Yeah, all right,' said the lad.

'I want one,' said the boy behind him. Within five minutes she had given out twelve tickets in the coffee line alone.

This was so risky. If Snell found out she was giving away tickets, she'd be done for. He'd say she was throwing money away, and then, most likely, throw her away too. She knew that he didn't care about sales, but he'd be glad of the excuse to get rid of Tig once and for all.

But they weren't really losing money. The theatre had been less than half full for all of Faber's shows so far, and empty seats were worth nothing. It was worth the risk.

She felt better already as she wove her way among the market stalls, picking out likely targets. The children who sold sweets and fruit outside the theatre were there with their barrow.

'Say, would you like to come and see the show tonight, after you finish selling?' Tig asked the girl.

'Dad says we 'ent got the money for that sort of thing.'

'Here you go.' She ripped off a strip of tickets. 'Bring your mam and daddy too.'

The little girl beamed and stuck out her hand. 'Thank you!'

'Tell everyone you're going! See you tonight.'

She stayed outside for another half-hour until all the tickets on the roll had gone.

Returning to the theatre, Tig managed to slip inside without anyone seeing her. She put the pound note the teacher had given her in the cash box. She was pleased with herself. Faber would have a good night tonight.

Between the free tickets, and the music school, and the punters who were going to show up anyway, it should guarantee a fairly full house for the show. Then people would *really* start talking about it, and would want to come and see the show for themselves. It always worked like that – popular shows got more and more popular, because everyone wanted to be part of the fun.

It would work. It had to work.

TICKETS

Eliza had asked Tig to help in the ticket booth that evening.

She brushed the dust off her coat, and pinned her hair back to look presentable. For the first time in a long while, there was a queue beginning to form outside the Royale when the doors opened at six thirty. People shuffled up to Tig's booth in twos and threes to show their tickets or buy seats.

'Is it true?' asked a woman in a large hat. 'Is it as clever as they say?'

'Indeed, madam,' said Tig. 'Truly a mechanical marvel.'

'It's not a trick, then?'

'Not a bit of it,' said Tig. 'I've inspected it myself.'

'Between you and me,' the lady leaned in conspiratorially. 'Is it worth the money?'

Tig nodded sagely. 'Most definitely. I've never seen such a wonder in all the world.'

The lady nodded and paid. A few moments later, two boys of around nine or ten were at the window.

'What's it like, then?' said the first one.

'We heard it's weird,' said the second.

'It's terrible,' said Tig, leaning forward and lowering her voice to a whisper. 'Monstrous.'

The boys grinned. 'Two, please.'

Amongst the last people to come through were the fruit-selling children and their parents. The father insisted on shaking Tig's hand through the window.

'Very kind,' he said. 'Very good of you indeed.'

He produced a huge orange from each pocket and placed them both on the counter.

'For you.'

Tig beamed, and tucked them away out of sight.

'Look at that, Edgar,' said Eliza as she closed up the front doors. 'A full house! The professor isn't a failure after all! Isn't that marvellous?'

156

'Yes. Marvellous.' Snell didn't look quite so thrilled. 'Won't you join me in the theatre, Eliza? I'd like to see the improved show for myself.'

'Why of course, dear brother.' Eliza took the arm that Snell had offered.

'And we can ensure there's no unscheduled appearances from any of the stage crew.'

Behind the Scenes

Tig watched the beginning of the show from the wings, delighted by the crowded house, and by Faber's pleasant surprise when he saw the size of the audience. It must've given him confidence, because he strode out onto the stage with his head held high, and remembered to project his voice, just as they'd practised.

Satisfied that the evening was going well, Tig seized the opportunity to sneak away and visit Nelson. The sickly-green worry inside her chest grew with every passing minute until it outweighed the feelings of shame – she had to check that he would be all right.

He lived down at the other end of the parish, in a dingy and miserable block of back-to-back houses. The buildings in this part of the city were small and cheap and dark, all crammed together tightly to squeeze in as many people as possible. They were built for the mill workers and all the underpaid, overworked poor who kept Manchester running.

The house Nelson shared with his grandmother and uncle faced into a little courtyard where three privies served fifty houses. The stench was thick as Tig passed through the ginnel and ducked under a washing line. Manchester was an overcrowded, industrial city, with a constant odour of horse manure and coal dust and fish markets, and the Royale itself often stank of sweat and dust and greasepaint. But nothing smelled quite as bad as the slums. They smelled of human misery.

She knocked on the front door and was let in by Nelson's grandmother, a lady scarcely older than Eliza but stooped and worn from endless hard labour. She had Nelson's wide smile and dark skin, and long hair pulled into a thick braid.

'Little Rabbit,' she said warmly. 'You haven't visited me in so long!'

Just as she had the first time they met, she flung her arms round Tig in a hug so warm and welcoming it almost made her forget her worries.

Coming here always brought up a mix of feelings for Tig. The dark, damp, uncomfortable house was a reminder of how lucky she was to live in the dry and spacious theatre. But at the same time, she was a little jealous of what Nelson had – a loving family who were always happy to see him at the end of the day.

Tig had spent many hours here since she moved to the Royale, sometimes helping with the mending work while

Nelson's grandmother told her about the adventures of her youth. When she was barely fifteen she had travelled by ship to England from the Americas, as a servant to a wealthy lady. En route she had fallen in love with a young sailor and when they reached land, they ran away together, eventually finding their way to Manchester. It was a grand love story, as good as any drama on stage at the Royale. It would make a wonderful play.

'Here he is, here he is,' Nelson's grandmother cooed. 'Tell him he needs to stay home and rest tomorrow. He won't hear it from me.'

Nelson was perched on a stool by the fire, cradling his bandaged hand to his chest. 'Can't afford to miss any more wages.'

The house had only two rooms – one downstairs, and one above. It shared three out of four walls with other homes, and the brickwork was thin so that the soft murmur of other families could be heard all the time. There was something peaceful about the sound, though Nelson often said crying babies and arguing neighbours made such a racket he couldn't sleep.

'How's your hand?'

'Ah, he was so tough when the doctor came,' said Nelson's grandmother. 'My brave boy.'

'Gran!' Nelson rolled his eyes, embarrassed.

'I brought you something.' Tig handed him one of the oranges the fruit-sellers had given her.

He grinned. 'Amazing! Thank you!'

'For being such a brave boy,' Tig added with a wink.

Nelson's grandmother took a jug down from a high shelf. 'I'm going to get your uncle's beer – he'll be home soon.'

'We'll go,' said Nelson. 'You don't mind, do you?'

'Course not.' Tig put her hand out for the beer jug.

'Well, if you're sure, I'll head up to bed. Don't dilly-dally, though. Goodnight, children,' said Gran, hauling herself up the narrow, uneven stairs with great difficulty.

'Night night.'

They set off into the street. Tig tried to breathe through her mouth to avoid the awful smell, but there was no escaping it.

'I'm really sorry you got hurt,' she said, unable to look Nelson in the eye.

'It's not your fault,' said Nelson. 'If Gus had just done his job, I wouldn't have been sawing wood in the first place.'

Guilt twisted her insides. 'Actually, it *was* my fault. I sent Gus out to buy paint.'

'Oh, right,' said Nelson. He looked hurt for a moment, then pulled together a smile. 'Well, you were just doing your job...'

'Ugh.' They crossed the road, hopping over a filthy puddle beside the kerb. 'No. I lied and made up a reason to get him out of the workshop.'

'What? Why?'

She stared at his injured hand. The bandage was wrapped so thickly around it that it looked like he was wearing mittens. 'Euphonia made another prediction.'

They stepped into the gutter to make room for a man pushing a coffee cart.

'She said that someone would get hurt in the workshop at three o'clock. Gus was the only one in there, so I thought if I could get rid of him before three o'clock, it wouldn't happen.'

'Oh, right.' Nelson held his bandaged hand to his chest. 'Why didn't you warn me?'

'I didn't know you'd come in and take over. I'm sorry.' *Sorry* didn't seem like a strong enough word. She wished she had been the one hurt instead. 'Faber told me not to interfere. But I couldn't do nothing.' She hopped over a puddle that was forming around a cracked flagstone.

Nelson furrowed his brow and looked down at his feet, deep in thought. 'How did we get mixed up in all this ghoulish stuff?'

'I don't know.'

'A few days ago all I was thinking about was what kind of meat pie to get on payday. That's the world I want to live in. Not this one with ghosts and machines and predictions.'

They walked in silence for a few hundred paces, then Tig gasped. With everything that was going on, she hadn't told him what had happened.

'Someone came to buy fifty tickets for the music school, and Snell sent him away! Told him we were all sold out. That's proof that he's trying to ruin the theatre.'

'Does Eliza know?'

'I haven't had chance to tell her yet. I chased the man down and sold the tickets anyway.' They paused as a labourer carried a bag of coal across the pavement in front of them. 'And Snell wasn't happy when the house was full tonight.'

'You got a full house? How?'

'I papered it – gave away tickets.'

'Snell's going to kill you if he finds out.'

'I know. But we're all doomed anyway, if the theatre closes.'

Doomed. She looked down at Uncle Lumpy's beer jug. Tig only had herself to look after. Nelson's whole family would suffer if the Royale closed.

'Well, we won't let it,' he said. 'We'll make sure people flock to see the talking machine, so it makes loads of money. In fact, we can start tonight.'

As they got nearer to the beerhouse, they passed a few of Nelson's neighbours on their way home. Everyone drank as much beer as they could afford around these parts – the water was often not very clean.

The beerhouse was really just a house. The main room had six or eight small round tables and each one was crowded with men. One or two women and a handful of children were present, but like Tig and Nelson they mostly waited with jugs to take drinks home. The sticky smell of old beer was a pleasant relief from the odours outside.

'Blimey, Nelson!' said a lanky boy in butcher's overalls. 'Been in a scrap?' He pointed to Nelson's bandaged hand.

'No,' said Nelson mysteriously. 'It was a curse.'

'Oh aye,' said the boy. He leaned back against the wall with a smile and folded his arms. 'Another Nelson story, eh? Come on, then, let's hear it.'

'I'll tell you for a pickled egg,' said Nelson.

'You're on,' said the boy. He passed his jug over for the landlord to fill, 'and an egg for the lad.'

'Careful, Nelson,' muttered Tig. 'What are you going to say about Faber?'

'Don't worry,' he whispered. 'They're just looking for a good story. No one expects the truth. Anyway, we said we was gonna chuck him a jolly, right?'

Most of the children in the queue, and a couple of men at the nearest tables, were already looking at Nelson – he clearly made a habit of sharing stories in exchange for snacks.

'Is it a theatre story?' said a small boy.

'That's right,' said Nelson. 'And do you know who's at the theatre now?'

The child shook his head.

'An inventor from far away across the seas.'

'As far as China?' said the boy.

'Further,' said Nelson. 'And he's brought with him a miraculous machine that talks with a human voice.'

'Speak up!' called someone from the back of the room.

Tig ordered Uncle Lumpy's ale while Nelson climbed up onto a stool. He wove a tale about the machine predicting the future, and how he was cursed because he made fun of it.

'I put my fingers in the machine's mouth,' said Nelson, holding up his bandaged hand. 'And it bit them almost clean off!' The men joined in, joking and encouraging him, while the children looked on in amazement.

In the midst of the noise, Tig looked around the room.

People were still coming in and out and by the door she thought she saw – *Gus*?

The boy had his cap pulled low over his face, and stood with his hands in his pockets.

What was he *doing* here? He lived on the other side of town and besides, he was supposed to be on curtain duty.

Had he followed them? Tig pushed her way through the crowd of other patrons, but by the time she reached the open door there was no sign of him.

She got back to Nelson's side just as he finished his tale. The landlord handed him a pickled egg, fished out of the huge jar of vinegar with his bare fingers.

'Get your cap off, boy,' said one of the men. He dropped a coin into Nelson's cap and within a minute several of the drinkers had done the same, and Nelson was rewarded with four and half-pence for his tale.

'That should get a few more of them in this week,' he said as they began the walk back home.

'I hope so,' said Tig, looking over her shoulder for Gus's shadow.

22

Exposition

Perhaps it was the satisfaction of getting a full house, or the relief at seeing Nelson wasn't too badly hurt, but Tig slept well that night, and deeply. She woke with a satisfied yawn and stretch.

Cold Annie was standing over her bed.

Tig yanked her fur-coat-blanket up to her face as if it could protect her from danger, then slowly relaxed. There was nothing to fear. Annie had been helping her.

'What is it?' asked Tig.

Annie turned and walked away, but disappeared before she reached the doorway. Tig dressed quickly and ran the length of the corridor, peering into each dressing room, but didn't find the ghost. How strange. What could she be trying to say?

As Tig reached the turn in the stairs, Annie was waiting at the bottom. Long strands of hair framed her face, floating as if stirred by a gentle breeze. Tig was pleased to see her there. How quickly one could get used to the most peculiar happenings – it almost felt normal to be in the company of a ghost now. Annie felt familiar, as if Tig had known her for years.

Annie turned away as Tig drew near. She crossed the workshop, leaving no footprints behind in the sawdust, and went through the doorway to the stage.

'Is something wrong?' she asked.

Annie walked to the centre of the stage, as she must have done many times in life. She stopped by Euphonia and stared directly at Tig with her one good eye.

'Euphonia,' said Tig. 'What about her? Do you know why she's talking?'

Cold Annie nodded, then disappeared.

'I don't understand!' Tig said to the empty air. She'd never had to solve a mystery before, and now there were mysteries everywhere, each one more baffling and frustrating than the last. It seemed as though she was getting nowhere.

But no, they had made progress. The full house last night, and Nelson's story at the beerhouse were sure to boost ticket sales. She just needed to stay focused.

'Knock knock.' She tapped on Faber's door.

'There is no need to say the word "knock" as well as knocking,' he said grumpily as he let her inside.

'Good morning, professor. What about last night's show, eh?' Tig sat down opposite him at the table. 'Full house!'

Faber smiled – actually smiled – and modestly looked down.

168

'I heard them talking on the way out. They loved you,' she continued. 'They were all really impressed.'

She decided not to mention the fact that everyone was most excited about how peculiar and unnerving the whole thing was. Nor did she mention that half of the tickets had been given away for free. He was pleased with himself, and that was something to celebrate.

'I got you a present,' said Tig. 'Close your eyes.'

'I will not.'

'Has anyone ever told you that you're no fun?'

'Yes,' said Faber.

She took out the second orange she'd been given last night, and laid it triumphantly on the table.

'What's that for?'

'It's food,' said Tig. 'You eat it.'

'I mean why—'

'It'll do you good. Stop you getting scurvy, or something.'

Faber ran his tongue over his teeth as if making sure they were all in place. He really was a strange and anxious man.

'Come on, eat it. It's delicious. And, it's all wrapped up in its own skin, so you don't need to worry about anyone touching it with their grubby hands.'

He reached out half-heartedly for the fruit, but then they were both distracted by a violent rapping at the door.

'What now?' demanded Faber as he yanked it open.

'Rabbit!' bellowed Mr Snell. 'My office. Now.'

Tig felt like a bucket of cold water had been tipped over her head. The panic must have shown on her face because

Faber silently followed them without being invited.

'This doesn't concern you, Mr Faber,' said Snell, in his usual simpering tone used for performers and paying guests. 'I can ask my sister to send some tea to your room, if you like.'

'This is my assistant, therefore it is my concern.' Faber spoke in a very matter-of-fact tone. Mr Snell looked flummoxed for a moment, then nodded and backed away.

In the office, Eliza sat in her armchair, chin resting on her hand. She looked serious, and concerned, which Tig found much more unsettling than Snell's anger.

Snell marched around his desk and stood behind it. He liked to do that before issuing orders and scoldings, to remind everyone who was the boss.

'Gus told me that you sent him out to pick up an order from Carter's.'

'I—'

'And that there was no order, Miss Rabbit. The whole thing was a lie.'

'It was . . . a misunderstanding,' said Tig.

'Do you think I need *you* to give orders? Do you want to run this theatre? Do you think you could do a better job?'

'No, sir.' She could *definitely* do a better job.

'So I had one boy sent home, and another wandering the city for no reason! You wasted valuable hours of work, and therefore, you wasted money.'

This wasn't a question so Tig just tried to look remorseful.

'But that's not the whole of it, is it?' said Snell. 'The money in the cash box is wrong. You're stealing from us.'

'No, I never!' Tig looked from Eliza to Faber to see if they believed her. Faber's expression was the same irritable one he always wore. Eliza shook her head sadly. 'I would never do that.'

'We had a full house last night. Saw it with my own eyes,' said Snell. 'Yet when my good sister counted up the cash box, we were thirteen shillings short.'

'Oh, Tig, pet, what have you done?' said Eliza, in a kind voice that cut like a knife. How could she think this of her?

'I can explain,' said Tig. 'I didn't steal anything. I gave away some tickets.'

'What, love?' said Eliza.

'You can search my things, check my pockets, look!' She turned out the pockets of her dress, dropping the contents onto Snell's desk: a pencil and paper, a loose button, a length of string, a box of pins, a small screwdriver and a tin of matches. 'I don't have the money. I gave out some tickets for free, so more people would come.'

Eliza was softening at this, but Snell only looked more angry. She could guess why.

'Giving away my property is stealing, Miss Rabbit,' said Snell. 'You've wasted all that income.'

'I haven't!' Tig said indignantly. She turned to Eliza for support. 'I haven't. Most of the people with free tickets brought friends, who paid for theirs! If it wasn't for the free tickets, we wouldn't have sold half as many.'

Tig glanced over at Faber, trying to read his face. She couldn't bear the thought of him considering her a thief.

'That's a fair point, Edgar,' said Eliza.

'Don't you start taking her side.'

'There were a lot of schoolboys in the audience last night.' Tig looked Snell directly in the eyes as she said this. It was a gamble. She was giving away the fact that she knew he had turned down the sale, and that she had gone behind his back to sell the tickets anyway. She'd already accused him of trying to sabotage the theatre, so she threw caution to the wind – in any case, there was no way he would dare admit what he'd been up to, not in front of Eliza. 'That's good news, isn't it, Mr Snell?' she said sweetly. 'That schoolmaster bought all those tickets – it made us eighteen shillings in one go.'

Snell stared back at her, face red and sweaty, nostrils flared. Tig kept her chin up and stared back defiantly.

'I've long had my doubts about you. I should have trusted my judgement. Eliza may be sentimental, but I am concerned only with business. I have no choice but to let you go.'

'But, Mr Snell, please—' This couldn't be happening. She was trying to help! Trying to save Gus an injury! Trying to save the theatre! And now she was going to be sent away from the place she loved so much. She was going to be penniless – homeless. She was going to have to work in a mill, if she was lucky enough not to simply end up on the streets.

'No.' Faber stepped forward.

Snell's eyes widened. 'With respect, Mr Faber, I have a business to run. I'm sure you would do the same in my position.'

'Eliza, please,' begged Tig.

'I don't know what to do with you any more, pet. Your behaviour has been so unpredictable lately...' She sighed, then leaned forward. 'I've been very patient with you, because of your family situation. But this has gone beyond what I can accept. Someone got *hurt*, Tig. This is serious.'

'You don't understand, I was trying to stop someone getting hurt. I can't explain. You need to trust me.' Her voice shook with the effort of staying calm. She tucked her hands under her armpits, trying to physically hold her feelings inside.

'And giving out those tickets, that wasn't your place.'

'But it worked!'

'You should have asked.'

'I would've asked, but you never listen to me!'

Eliza put her hand to her chest in surprise. Tig was too worked up to care about hurting the woman's feelings. This was stupid. Because she was just twelve, just a stagehand, *just a girl* she was expected to obey the grown-ups in charge, even when the grown-ups were wrong.

'Out of kindness,' said Snell, 'I will let you sleep here tonight, and you can find somewhere else to go in the morning.'

No. No no no no no.

'I cannot be without my assistant.' Faber folded his arms.

'I assure you, the boys will step up and assist you.'

'No. It must be this girl. She knows how to care for the machine.'

'Miss Rabbit has caused no end of trouble with her actions.' Mr Snell was beginning to raise his voice.

'She said it was a misunderstanding. Is that not enough?' demanded Faber.

'I can't afford to pay someone to cause misunderstandings.'

'Then I will pay for her.' He reached into his pocket and flung a handful of coins onto the desk. Tig followed a shilling with her eyes as it rolled off the table and circled round and round on the floor. 'I can't imagine you pay her more than that. Don't think I haven't noticed how you treat her. I've seen where she sleeps.'

Tig's cheeks flushed red.

'I . . . well . . .' Mr Snell was clearly shocked. His expression flickered from embarrassment to discomfort to anger. He was obviously frustrated by Faber's unusual behaviour.

Snell frowned and looked from Faber to Tig and back again. 'Miss Rabbit,' he said quietly. 'Please wait outside while the adults are talking.'

Tig walked out of the room, fuming. Mr Snell followed behind her and closed the door firmly. She listened with her ear to the door, but the wood was thick and the voices were muffled so she gave up and flopped down onto the bottom step, head in hands.

Was this what Annie had been trying to tell her that morning? That she was about to be fired?

No, that didn't make sense. It was something to do with the machine, that much was clear. Was she warning her to listen to the predictions or . . .

A spark flickered.

Cold Annie and Euphonia weren't two different mysteries

at all. They were one and the same.

Raised voices spilled out from the office but Tig barely noticed. How had she missed this?

Faber said that Euphonia had never spoken on her own before. The very first time was the night he arrived at the Royale, after Tig had met Cold Annie in the flies and damaged the talking machine. Annie had led her to the red coat with the glass eye in the pocket, and given her the idea to fix it.

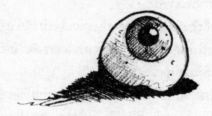

A shiver swept through her, toe to scalp. Cold Annie was making the machine talk!

The stalls door opened, startling Tig from her thoughts. Nelson came through carrying a broom and humming to himself. He really ought to be home and resting, but Tig had never been more pleased to see him.

'Nelson!' She ran across the tiles to meet him. 'I've worked it out. The machine isn't talking at all. It's Cold Annie. She's making it talk. She's using it, somehow, to give us messages.'

'What?'

'Annie made me drop the light-stick and break Euphonia's eye. Annie showed us where the new eye was. And once her eye was in the machine, it could speak by itself! It all makes sense!'

Nelson looked doubtful. 'Sort of, I suppose.' He rested his elbow on top of his broom and frowned.

'But it still doesn't explain how she knows the future.'

'Maybe it does,' said Nelson. 'Remember? My cousin said when Annie was alive she could always predict when a performance was going to go wrong.'

'Yes!' Tig hugged him, hard. The broom clattered to the floor. 'I was right then. Cold Annie, Euphonia – they're *both* trying to help us. To warn us of bad things happening at the theatre.'

'Have you told the professor?'

'He's . . .' Everything came back with a crash. 'It's too late, Nelson. Snell is firing me.'

Right on cue the office door opened. Tig put her shoulders back and gritted her teeth. She would look Snell in the eye, and not give him the pleasure of seeing her upset.

'Miss Rabbit,' said Snell. 'It seems Mr Faber feels very strongly that your work is invaluable to him.'

'*Professor* Faber,' said Tig under her breath.

Snell glared, his nostrils flaring. 'And as he is our valued guest, I will allow you to remain in your position. You will be docked three days' wages for the trouble you have caused. And make no mistake, there will be no more chances. We are all in agreement.' He leaned in, his lips so close to her ear that she could feel his hot, damp breath. 'Faber and Eliza can't protect you for ever, you irritating little girl. I'll be rid of you the first chance I get.'

'Thank you, Mr Snell,' said Tig. She even added a little

curtsey. That had been close. Too close.

'What are you standing about for, boy?!' Snell directed his frustration at Nelson. 'Get back to work, idle creature!'

'Come along, Miss Rabbit,' said Faber.

23

Foreshadowing

'What did you say to change his mind?' Tig demanded, as soon as she and Professor Faber were out of Snell's earshot.

'I said either you stay, or I go.' He brushed a speck of dust from his sleeve. 'It was Eliza who agreed, in the end. She said the Royale couldn't afford to lose me, now we were making good sales.'

But, Tig reminded herself, Faber was only due to be at the Royale for a month at most. Soon he would be gone, and then who would stop Snell from firing her?

'Thank you,' said Tig.

Faber nodded. They entered the Green Room, and he took up his usual seat next to his notebook and pens.

'I want you to promise me that next time the machine makes a prediction—'

'It's not the machine!' Tig blurted out. 'I figured it out. It's our theatre ghost, she's making it talk.'

Breathlessly she explained her theory and everything they knew about Cold Annie and her habit of predicting misfortune. Faber's face showed first confusion, then concern, and then relief. It settled, in the end, on disappointment. He closed his notebook with a decisive snap.

Tig stopped talking. She'd been so excited to finally have some clue about what was happening, she'd been sure the professor would be as pleased as she was. Now she saw that it meant something else to him. He had hoped that he had somehow built a miracle machine. By some accidental genius he had invented a device that spoke the future, something beyond imagination. Tig's revelation had taken that away.

'Do you believe me?' she said gently.

'I believe in science. Logic. Facts.' He rubbed his eyes. 'It seems none of those have any meaning in this place.'

For once, Tig couldn't think of anything to say.

'Whatever the cause,' said Faber at last. 'If she makes another prediction you will not try to fix it or prevent it.'

'But—'

'No. We have seen that we cannot stop the predictions coming true. Your attempts have only made things worse. I don't want anyone else hurt. And I'm not certain I can keep Mr Snell from dismissing you if there's any more trouble.'

Tig suddenly felt a lump in her throat and exhaustion washed over her. It felt like she was adrift at sea, the waves lifting her high one moment, then crashing through her the next, threatening to drag her under. The theatre was safe for now, but everything else was getting worse. Next time, someone could be killed. 'Well then ... if we can't stop it ourselves, we need to tell someone. We need help.'

'Absolutely not. If people find out they will want her, take her away. I can't allow that to happen.' He patted his pockets down until he found his box of health pills.

'Professor ... I can't listen to her predicting horrible things and not try and stop them. I just can't. I won't.'

Faber sighed and swallowed a handful of pills.

'Whatever is happening here, I'm right in the middle of it,' Tig continued. 'You can't expect me to pretend nothing is happening.'

'I can tell Mr Snell to find me a new assistant!'

Tig folded her arms and stamped her foot. Why were adults always so difficult? 'You've just fought to stop me from being fired.'

That deflated him. 'Of course I'm not going to. Even though, truth be told, you are the most troublesome child.'

Tig rolled her eyes, but said nothing. Sometimes making trouble was the only way to get things done.

'Euphonia said I can trust you, and she's been right about everything else so far.' Faber paced from one end of the room to the other, taking big, energetic strides. 'I find myself restless. There's no air in this place.'

'Why don't you go for a walk outside? It's nice weather. You've plenty of time before the show.'

'I can't leave the machine. Someone might interfere with

her. Or she might speak again, and someone will overhear.'

'I'll stay with her,' offered Tig. 'I'll sit in the theatre and make sure no one touches her.'

Faber tilted his head to the side.

'Well . . . I suppose a short stroll, not too far. If you're sure you'll stay with her.'

'I'd much rather stay in here, out of the way of Snell and Gus.'

'Very well.' He puffed out his chest as if bracing himself to do something dangerous and scary. 'I will go for a walk.'

'Good for you!'

'And you will . . .' He nodded towards the machine.

'I'll protect her with my life. I promise.'

Tig broke the promise four minutes later.

She really, *really* didn't mean to. For the first three minutes she lay on the stage, staring up at the beams overhead, daydreaming about all the reporters that would come if they knew about Euphonia's magic, and how the Royale would be the most famous theatre in the country. Snell would be thwarted once and for all.

But then Euphonia started to speak.

'**So much fuel to burn. The sudden spark. The black smoke. Your friend must run.**'

The machine fell silent, the final note lingering in the empty theatre like dust. Tig's fingers were shaking as she scrabbled for her pencil and paper to write down Euphonia's words.

She wasn't going to act on them. She mustn't.

But this sounded awful.

Follow the rabbit through the flames – that's what the machine had said the first night. And now she was talking about fire again. The two *must* be connected – perhaps she, Tig, was destined to stop a fire!

Who was the friend? Surely not Nelson again? He was sweeping in the foyer – no risk of fire there. And Gus certainly wasn't her friend. They'd never said a friendly word to each other and he'd been trying to get her into trouble for days. Faber was out. Eliza didn't seem so friendly towards her any more.

The only other person she could almost call a friend was . . . Matilde.

The chemist shop.

The signs Mr Becker had put outside were advertising fireworks. He was making fireworks, himself, inside.

They used gunpowder for that – the same stuff that fired cannons. It was horribly explosive. Matilde had said that the tiniest spark—

Tig had to warn them!

She'd promised Faber that she'd stay with the machine, but this was more important. *Surely even he would agree?* she thought, sprinting up the aisle.

'What's the hurry, dear?' said Eliza as Tig barrelled past her in the foyer. But there was no time to explain.

On the pavement she hopped from foot to foot waiting for a break in the traffic. Last time she had been too hasty, leaving before the clock struck three. If she took her time, and made absolutely certain, she could make sure it would be different.

Darting between two wagons she raced across the road and shoved the chemist's door open. The bell above it jangled.

Matilde looked up from the ledger she was writing in and smiled. 'Tig!' She came out from behind the counter and headed over towards her.

'Fireworks!' panted Tig. 'Is Mr Becker making fireworks today?'

'No, why?'

'I can't really explain.' Tig leaned against the shelves to catch her breath. 'But you mustn't.'

'What?'

'If you make fireworks today, there's going to be a fire.'

Matilde knitted her brows together. 'Papa's been making fireworks for years. We've never had an accident yet.'

'I know,' said Tig. 'But please trust me. Whatever happens, you mustn't let anyone make fireworks today, or else something awful will happen.'

'You needn't worry,' said Matilde. 'We're not working on them today. Mama and I are balancing the books and Papa is making—'

Right on cue, Mr Becker bustled out from the back room. 'Here you are again, Miss Rabbit, distracting my daughter when she is meant to be working, and no doubt so are you.' He began ushering her towards the door.

'No,' said Tig. 'I needed to give you an important message.'

'Oh?' said the chemist, but before Tig could explain they

were interrupted by a thick column of black smoke from the back room.

Mr Becker let out an alarmed grunt and ran towards the source of the smoke.

'Oh no,' said Tig. 'You said you weren't making fireworks today.'

'He's making matches,' said Matilde.

'The sand buckets!' shouted Mr Becker from within. Matilde ran for the big metal bucket full of damp sand that had been placed by the door, and Tig followed with a second from the end of the counter. They passed them in turn to Mr Becker who dumped out the sand onto the smouldering work bench. Dirty black scorch marks had already appeared on the wall above, but the fire was out.

'What happened, Papa?' asked Matilde, as she brought out the dustpan and broom from the cupboard.

'I was distracted from my work by you two wastrels.' He pointed at Tig. 'You! Out! I've had enough of you causing trouble round here.'

'I was trying—'

'Out!'

She'd failed. Again. Four predictions. Three accidents caused by her interference and one – the carriage – by their inaction.

This time there might have been no accident at all if Tig hadn't run into the chemist and distracted Mr Becker.

Faber was right. Perhaps she should have ignored Euphonia, and so the accidents wouldn't have happened. But then why would Euphonia predict them in the first place?

Tig's thoughts were taking her round and round in circles and with each loop she got more confused and uncomfortable. She sat on the steps outside the milliner's and took a few deep breaths. Going back into the theatre, to possibly hear more words in that unearthly voice, filled her with dread. For the first time ever, she wanted to be anywhere else but the Royale.

She watched the people mill back and forth on their way to and from work, stopping to buy baked potatoes or talk to a friend in the street. It was a sea of grey, despite the sunshine. The roads were grey and filthy with horsemuck. The buildings were grey with soot from the factories. Even the people were grey in their dull, practical cloaks and shawls. Men strode by in their identical top hats . . .

Faber!

The professor was coming round the corner.

Back already. Tig jumped up and pushed her way through the stream of people, running back to the theatre. If the professor realized she had left his precious machine unattended the very first time he had trusted her with it, he'd be furious.

She raced up the stairs, ran across the foyer, and burst panting into the auditorium.

Euphonia was there, exactly as she had been left. Of course.

Although – was it Tig's imagination? – it seemed like Euphonia was at a slightly different angle to before, and out of the corner of her eye she was sure she saw the backdrop cloth swaying slightly as though somebody had brushed against it.

She listened carefully for footsteps, but heard nothing. Quickly she got herself into position, sitting on the stage, and fought to get her breath back so Faber would never know she had been running. Less than a minute later, Faber entered. She was just in time.

'Back already?' she asked with a smile.

'The air in this city doesn't agree with me,' he said, striding across the stage and removing his hat. 'I need my throat tonic from my room.'

Tig lay back on the boards of the stage, staring up into the flies above, and thought about Matilde. They'd never be proper friends, now.

'Ahhh!' A sudden loud yell, almost a scream, came from Faber's room. Tig hurtled in to find Faber standing in the opposite doorway, horror painted across his features.

The room had been ransacked.

The Green Room

The drawers of the dressing table were open, the chairs had been pulled out and left at odd angles and the professor's clothes were dumped in a pile in the middle of the room. His carpet bag had been tipped out, leaving combs and pencils and boot polish in a careless pile. The doorway to Faber's bedroom was wide open; blankets were strewn across the floor and his mattress had been flipped over.

In the midst of the wreckage stood Faber, paler than Cold Annie.

'What happened?' he stammered.

'I don't know,' said Tig.

'Euphonia, is she—'

'She's fine.'

He crossed the room in four steps and pushed past her to see for himself.

Tig followed him. How could this have happened? They had only been gone for a few minutes, at the most.

A moment later Snell's sweaty face appeared. 'I heard shouting. What's the matter?'

Faber threw his hands up. 'What do you think is the matter?' He pointed Snell towards the Green Room.

'Oh my. Oh my, my.' Snell held onto the doorframe.

'Who did this?' Faber demanded. 'Has one of your boys been in here?'

'I assure you I can vouch for all of my men,' said Snell. 'Everyone is hard at work aside from . . .' He gestured towards Tig.

'I only stepped out for a moment,' said Tig. 'Have we been burgled?' She hadn't locked the doors behind her when she ran out to the chemist, but it'd take a bold thief to walk right in from the street. 'The takings! Did they get—'

'Be quiet, Miss Rabbit,' said Snell. 'I was in the office the entire time. Nobody came through the lobby.'

She felt a moment of relief – the Royale certainly couldn't afford to lose a night's takings – but it was followed immediately by worry. Who would come into the building, and go straight to Faber's room to search it? Who, outside the theatre, would even know their way around backstage, or know that Faber lived in the Green Room?

'Was anything stolen?' asked Snell.

'I don't know yet.' Faber picked up his jacket and patted it down. 'My watch. My pocket watch is gone.'

Tig's heart was pounding so hard that it made her whole body quake.

'I was only gone for a second,' she said again. 'I didn't see anyone come out.'

'What are you standing there for?' said Faber to Snell. 'Search the building. The thief may still be here!'

'Of course. Gus!' he yelled, bustling out of the room. 'Search the building! Mr Faber's been robbed!' His voice echoed up the corridor as he retreated.

That just left Tig and Faber.

'I can explain,' she began.

'I don't want to hear excuses.' Faber's jaw was clenched tight as he began picking up his belongings. He laid his comb and his pencils on the dresser at neat, precise angles.

'At least Euphonia is all right,' said Tig quietly.

Faber closed a drawer with a thud.

Somehow the professor's silence was worse than if he had shouted at her. He shook out a blanket and threw it onto the bed. Tig hurried to smooth it out.

'You were trying to stop another prediction coming true, weren't you?' he said at last.

'I . . .' Tig hesitated. She wasn't sure if it was better to admit it, or if that would only make him more frustrated after his repeated warnings not to listen to the machine.

'Well?'

'Euphonia said there was going to be a fire in the chemist. They have a barrel of gunpowder for making fireworks. Me and Nelson know the girl there, I – I couldn't let her get hurt.'

'And?' He crouched down to pick up the carpet bag. 'Did you stop it?'

'No. I made it happen.'

Anger and alarm radiated from him like heat from a candle flame.

'I'm sorry.'

He straightened up suddenly, throwing aside the remaining clothes, and twisted around to look behind him. 'They're gone.'

'What are?'

'My plans. The plans for Euphonia, and all my notes,' Panic was written across his face.

Tig joined him in searching the Green Room.

'You didn't see anyone?' He looked beneath the chaise. 'Think, girl! Think!'

'I didn't see anything!'

'You promised me that you would stay and watch the machine.'

'I had no choice!'

'Of course you had a choice. We always have a choice.'

'It was the right thing to do.'

'The right thing was to keep your promise, and ignore the predictions. You've made everything worse.'

Snell returned, sticking his red face around the doorframe. 'The building has been searched, Mr Faber. There's no one here. Probably some street beggar child who saw the open door.'

'The plans for my machine have been taken,' said Faber. 'Does that seem like something a street child would want?'

Tig took the opportunity to skulk away, slipping through

the door to the stage. She leaned back against the wall, trying to make sense of everything that had happened in the last half an hour.

Whoever the thief was, they had broken in on the very first occasion that both Faber and Tig were out of the theatre. That couldn't just be lucky timing. Somebody must be watching them. But who? Could it be someone who worked at the Royale? Why would they want Faber's plans? And had they heard Euphonia's prediction?

'You could have warned me, Euphonia,' said Tig under her breath. 'Or Annie. Whoever you are.'

On the other side of the door Faber and Snell were still engaged in tense conversation.

'Just one of those things. We've never had a break-in before. Terrible luck—' Snell was saying.

'The loss of my life's work is hardly "one of those things", Mr Snell,' replied Faber. 'Get out. Leave me alone. We will discuss this later.'

Once Snell left, Faber emerged from the Green Room. Without saying a word to Tig, he crossed to Euphonia and stood at one end. He snapped his fingers and pointed to the other end of the machine, then lifted its side so the legs came up off the ground.

Tig went to pick up the machine without complaint. In silence they carried it into the Green Room, Faber walking backwards, and set it down against the wall. 'You can go now.'

Waiting in the Wings

Ten minutes before the show was due to begin that evening, Faber still hadn't emerged from his room.

Tig tapped on the Green Room door.

'Professor, it's Tig. The audience are waiting.'

There was a scraping noise and finally the door opened. Once inside she saw that he had rearranged the furniture – it looked as though he had been barricading the door with the dressing table.

'I'm not going out there.'

'You have to. We'll lose a lot of money if you don't.'

Faber shrugged. 'I have enough.'

'How nice for you.' Tig folded her arms. 'And what about the rest of us, hmm? You think we can afford to run this place with no shows?'

Faber looked like he was about to answer, then he closed his mouth.

Tig knew she should stop talking. But after everything that had happened in the last few days – most of the chaos beginning, one way or another, with Faber's machine – she didn't have the will to contain herself.

'In a few weeks you'll be gone. But we'll still be here. I'll still be here. If you lose us money we won't be able to afford to put the next show on. What happens to me, to Nelson, to all of us?'

Faber looked a little taken aback at this rant. He let out an irritated sigh and stood up. She was sure he was about to show her out and slam the door, but before he had the chance to do anything, Euphonia spoke.

'**A quarter to nine precisely the theatre thief will strike again**.'

Tig gasped. 'Quarter to nine. Something's going to be stolen during your show!'

'Enough!' Faber roared. 'Will you never learn?'

Angry tears bubbled up and threatened to spill over. She took a deep breath. 'I'm sorry someone took your plans. I'm sorry I didn't keep better guard. But at least I was doing it for a good reason. You only care what happens to *you*. You won't help when the machine says someone is in danger and you won't even get up on stage and do your actual job.'

The professor rubbed his hand across his face. 'Fine. I'll do the show.'

'Thank—'

'On the condition that you don't try to stop that prediction. I want you to sit in the wings so I can see you during the show, and know you're not going to get yourself hurt again.'

Tig considered this. She was desperate to do something about the prediction, for the sake of the theatre and everyone in it. But having Faber performing would help the theatre too, and there was a certain relief in having an excuse not to intervene this time – the last few times had gone so badly.

'Agreed,' she said.

'Hurry up, then.'

She lifted the other end of the machine and between them they carried it out into the centre of the stage.

'One minute to curtain!' came Gus's voice from the corner of the stage as he took his place by the curtain ropes.

Tig and Faber went into the wings.

'Stay here,' whispered Faber as the curtains rose. 'Exactly on this spot.' He strode out onto the stage and the audience applauded.

'Ladies and gentlemen,' he began in a loud, clear voice.

It was Faber's best show yet. The audience loved him, and clapped and laughed in all the right places. When the curtain finally fell at nine o'clock, Tig rushed to congratulate him. They peered inside the Green Room somewhat nervously – it was after a quarter to nine – but nothing seemed to have been taken. Everything was exactly as they had left it. Faber looked relieved as Tig bade him goodnight.

But when Tig emerged into the lobby to close up, she

found a commotion. Snell and Eliza were standing in the middle of a group of ten or twelve patrons, all talking at once and looking very angry.

'Tig!' shouted Eliza over the din. 'Run and get the Peelers. We've had a pickpocket.'

26

Deus Ex Machina

Emerging into the cool evening air, Tig wanted to scream and scream and scream. It seemed she couldn't win.

She went to the corner of Fountain Street and York Street to look for a police officer. The Peelers, as people called them, always walked the same routes at the same time every day, so people always knew where to find them if they needed help.

Unfortunately, the thieves knew their routes as well, and were sure to do any thieving and burgling when the Peelers weren't around. She waited for the distinctive dark blue uniform and tall hat to come into view and ran to tell him what had happened. He barked a gruff thanks and set off running towards the Royale, but Tig knew it was too late. The pickpocket would be long gone by now.

Tig watched anxiously as each of the victims took their

turn telling the policeman what was stolen. Everyone was very angry, and several were loudly blaming the Royale staff for allowing this to happen. It was the last thing they needed.

'I want my ticket refunded,' said one man.

'Yes, of course,' Eliza said. 'We're very sorry this has happened to you. All of you will have your money refunded.'

'And what about the money what was nicked?' another man shouted. 'I reckon you should be paying us that, too! It's your fault for letting in a thief! Wasn't nobody watching?'

'Everything seems to be in hand here,' Snell declared loudly. 'I'm just stepping out, Eliza.'

'What? Now?'

'A quick drink or two. To settle my nerves. I've had a hard day.'

He didn't look like a man having trouble with his nerves. He looked excited. He kept his head low as he pushed his way through the mob and out of the front doors, but Tig was sure she detected the hint of a smile. Takings had been good tonight for the first time, but this would cost them a lot of money. Quite a stroke of luck for Snell.

Luck? Or planning?

Would he stoop so low as to hire a criminal at his own theatre?

She leaned against the wall heavily.

'Hey, Tig?' It was Nelson. 'You don't look well.'

'I'm fine,' she said. 'I'm tired. This week has been too much.'

'You need sleep,' said Nelson. 'You go up to bed. I'll do the theatre lights, and I'll lock up once this lot leave.'

'Are you sure?' The thought of escaping to the quiet of her own space was so tempting.

'Of course. Go. Sleep.'

But she couldn't sleep. Whenever she closed her eyes she saw Snell's unbearable smirk. She had fixed Faber's show *and* got the audiences coming in. She had beaten him, and yet somehow, he was still winning. They had to get him out of the Royale completely, before he had chance to ruin them.

After a lot of tossing and turning, she got back up, and walked downstairs in her nightgown and bare feet. She crept onto the stage and stood in front of Euphonia. She felt silly, but she didn't know what else to do. Soft snores came from the direction of the Green Room, but the building was otherwise silent.

'Euphonia.' She kept her voice low, so as not to wake the professor. 'Or Annie, if you're there. Help me. Tell me what I'm supposed to do now.'

Nothing.

'Please?'

Of course it didn't work. She turned to leave.

'**Betrayal.**' It was quieter than usual, a creaking whisper, as if the machine didn't want to wake anyone either. '**Betrayal at the theatre.**'

Tig marched back out to the middle of the stage. 'Betrayal!' she hissed at the machine. 'What sort of a prediction is that? I already know that Snell's been betraying us all along!'

Euphonia stayed silent.

'I need more,' Tig pleaded. 'I know about the betrayal, but Eliza won't listen and I don't have any proof! If you expect me to stop him, you need to help me. You need to tell me, in plain words, what to do!'

Tig started to shiver. It was cold. Much colder than it had been a few moments before. Did that mean...?

When she turned around, Cold Annie was right behind her. Immediately the ghost stepped forward, passing right through Tig like an icy wind. Annie headed to the back of the stage, and down the steps to hell.

She followed.

Without a candle to light her way, Tig had to shuffle slowly through hell, feeling with fingers and toes for obstacles in her path. Cold Annie waited in the opposite corner, and as Tig got closer, she headed into the storage rooms and then beyond, to the door to Eliza and Snell's apartment.

Annie walked right through the door. Tig hesitated. She had no idea what time it was – whether Eliza would still be awake, or whether Snell was back home from the pub. Slowly she turned the handle, easing the door open as softly as she could.

The kitchen was empty. The door to Eliza's room was closed, and Snell's stood open. He was still out. Cold Annie went into Snell's bedroom, but by the time Tig got there, she had vanished.

'Is there something here?' whispered Tig. 'What am I looking for?'

Snell's favourite suit was draped over the high-backed

wooden chair in the corner and his musky cologne lingered in the air.

Nothing seemed unusual or out of place. His Sunday shoes were neatly tucked beneath the bed, with his chamber pot – thankfully empty. A handful of creams and ointments lay beside the wash basin. A box of candles sat on a chest of drawers.

There must be something here. Some proof of his betrayal and his plot against Eliza and the Royale. She opened the drawers one at a time, but found nothing except the usual collection of socks and shirts and spare bootlaces. Nothing.

But underneath one corner was a scrap of creamy white paper. She picked it up. There was writing on this one, but she couldn't tell what it said, because it was written in German.

It was from Faber's notebook. It must have fallen out, and Snell hadn't noticed it tucked away beneath the furniture legs.

Tig began frantically searching the room for the rest of Faber's plans. There was nothing under the bed, or concealed between the pillows.

She even put her hands in the pockets of all his clothes, hoping to find something. The plans and note were not here, but they had been – the scrap of paper was proof. Did Snell think stealing them would make Faber want to leave the Royale? Or had he somehow found out about the predictions?

Should she wake Eliza now, and show her the evidence while Snell wasn't around? No, she'd go to Faber first. After all the trouble Tig had been in lately, Eliza would be more likely to listen to him.

Snell was standing in the doorway.

'Rabbit,' he sneered.

'Mr Snell.' She had to think fast. 'I was looking for my . . . ah . . . my pins. I had a box of pins. I thought I might've left them here when I was helping Eliza mend her dress earlier.'

There was a darkness in his eyes. He was angry, but it wasn't his usual, blustery, self-important anger. This was cold and sharp and controlled.

'You were snooping through my private things. What's that in your hand?'

'Nothing,' said Tig, placing her hands behind her back.

He held out his hand.

She reluctantly passed over the paper, hoping she could buy some time to think of a way out.

He unfolded it. They stood in silence for a moment, as though sizing up their situation.

'I know you stole Faber's plans,' said Tig, sounding braver than she felt. 'You need to return them to him, now.'

Snell's scowl became a smirk. 'Do I really?'

'Otherwise I'll tell everyone and Eliza will kick you out of here.'

Snell paused. A smile slowly crept across his face. 'Excellent idea, Miss Rabbit. Let's wake them all. Eliza!' he shouted.

27

Upstaged

What was Snell doing? It didn't make sense!

'Come with me,' he said, grabbing Tig by the wrist. 'Eliza! Mr Faber!'

'Let go of me,' said Tig.

'No, no,' replied Snell. 'You know best, as always, Tig Rabbit. Let's wake the whole theatre and let everyone know what's been going on around here.'

She tried to pull away from him, but his grip was too tight.

'Give him his plans back,' said Tig defiantly. 'And stop trying to sell the theatre.'

'The plans are long gone, Tig. I had no trouble finding a buyer. A machine that can tell the future? Those plans fetched me a pretty penny.'

Tig's heart sank. The professor's fears had come true. 'What are you talking about? The machine can't tell the future.'

'Too late to deny it. Gus saw it.'

'Nothing can tell the future. That snooping toad is wrong.' She twisted her arm back and forth.

They moved through the apartment and as they reached the exit, Eliza emerged bleary-eyed from her room, bedjacket around her shoulders.

'Edgar? Whatever is the matter?'

'So sorry to disturb you, dear,' he said in a falsely jolly tone of voice. 'Could you possibly join us upstairs? I'm afraid it's rather important.'

He opened the door to the stairs and gave Tig a poke in the back.

'Up you go,' he said. 'Let's find your precious professor and tell him what happened to his plans.'

'You won't get away with this.'

Snell dragged Tig all the way to the Green Room and hammered on the door.

'Mr Faber!' he shouted again.

Faber's door opened slightly. Unlike Eliza, it did not look like he had been sleeping.

'Professor,' snapped Faber, but he opened the door a little wider. 'It's about the break-in.'

The professor glanced from Snell to Tig and frowned. 'Let go of her, at once.'

Snell handed the scrap of paper to Faber. 'I found this in Miss Rabbit's possession.'

Faber unfolded the paper. 'This is . . .'

'Clearly from your book of plans. The book wasn't with

her – she has probably sold it already. And this.' Snell reached into his inside pocket and pulled out a pocket watch. Faber's pocket watch.

'My watch!' Faber grabbed it out of Snell's hands.

Eliza caught up with them, squinting sleepily.

'I regret to inform you that Miss Rabbit is the thief,' announced Snell.

'No!' shouted Tig.

'She will of course be dismissed from our employment immediately.'

'Tig,' said Eliza. 'How could you?' She put her hand to her mouth, upset.

'He's lying!' she pleaded. 'Mr Snell has—'

'I should have guessed. She was the only one who had access to your room and her behaviour lately has been so erratic. I can only apologize—'

'Professor, this isn't true,' said Tig. She stepped towards him. 'I found—'

'Be quiet, Miss Rabbit,' said Faber.

Tig fell into a horrified silence. How could he believe Snell? It felt like one of the stage trapdoors had opened beneath her and she was falling, falling. Not just into the space beneath the stage, but through an endless pit of darkness.

'Miss Rabbit had my watch because I gave it to her,' Faber said.

'What?' said Snell, flustered. 'No, you misunderstand, Mr Faber. This is the watch that was stolen from your room. I found it, in Miss Rabbit's belongings.'

'I asked her to get it repaired.' Professor Faber's eyes met Tig's for a moment and the slightest twitch in his expression told her that she should play along.

'But...' Snell held a polite smile on his face but his eyes flicked around the room – he was wrong-footed by Faber's unexpected reaction. 'The burglary...'

'Yes, the burglary. The shock of it caused me to forget, briefly, that I had instructed her to take the watch to be fixed.' He flipped open the cover. 'Ah yes. Seems to be working now. Well done, Miss Rabbit.'

'Well done, Edgar. What a tremendous waste of everyone's time.' Faber bowed in her direction. 'I apologize for the confusion. I did not mean to cause any difficulties.'

'But, the paper.'

'This trifle?' The professor shrugged and crumpled the paper. 'It is nothing. A list I wrote when I was packing. No doubt she meant to throw it away and forgot about it.'

Tig nodded furiously.

Snell's face was becoming redder and his whole posture was stiff. He seemed, for once, lost for words.

Tig bit her lip, enjoying watching Snell squirm. He knew they were lying, but what could he say? To expose them would be to admit that he'd stolen the plans and the watch.

'I trust this is the end of the matter,' Faber added. 'It is very late, and I do not wish to be disturbed again.' He went back into his room and slammed the door.

'What is going on around here lately?' demanded Eliza. 'I'm getting thoroughly fed up of all these goings on.'

'All this could have been avoided,' said Snell, pointing a finger at Tig. 'If she had spoken up about the watch. It's a form of dishonesty, if you ask me. Disturbing you in the middle of the night over nothing, Eliza.'

He was flustered, trying to cover his tracks and shift the blame.

'I think you'll find it was you that disturbed us in the middle of the night,' said Eliza.

'You're always looking for some way to blame me,' said Snell. 'I've said all along . . .'

Their bickering faded away as they retreated back in the direction of their rooms.

Tig felt a wave of relief wash over her. The professor had believed her. He still trusted her.

28

On Cue

Tig was up at the crack of dawn the next morning, but by the time she got downstairs, Faber was already awake.

'Snell knows,' she said. 'He told me last night. He knows Euphonia predicts the future.'

'How did he find out?'

'Gus has been spying on us.'

'I see. Well, that settles it, then. I cannot stay here any longer.' He retrieved his carpet bag from its corner and put it on the table to begin packing.

'You're leaving?'

'Of course I am. Now, don't do that.'

'Do what?'

'The sad face.'

'I'm not doing it on purpose,' said Tig. 'I *am* sad. If you go, what happens to us lot, here? We haven't made enough money yet. The theatre will probably close and be sold.'

'I'm sorry, but I can't stay where Euphonia is at risk.'

As if she had been listening for the right moment, Euphonia began to speak.

'The day is here. The rescuer comes and the fire begins. Two hundred souls inside.'

'I do not like the sound of that,' said Tig.

'Oh no, oh goodness.' Faber pressed his knuckles into his temples.

Tig took out her paper and unfolded her notes with all of Euphonia's prophesies written down. She snatched up Faber's pen and added this new prediction to her list.

'A fire. There's going to be another fire – two hundred people! You can't ignore this one.'

'No, I'm not listening to you.' Faber shook his head. 'I will not intervene in Euphonia's predictions. Every time you have been involved, it has made things worse.'

'What's worse than two hundred people in a fire? Please, you have to help me stop this.'

He reached for one of his medicine bottles. Tig watched closely as he measured out a dose of the sticky red syrup. It was very slight, but she noticed it – his hands were shaking. He was frightened.

Swallowing the medicine, the professor reached into his waistcoat pocket and pulled out the crumpled paper from the night before. He put it on the desk and smoothed it out carefully.

Lines and lines of writing in Faber's skinny, angular script. Most of them were crossed out with a single strike but four were not.

'You have a list, too,' said Tig. 'It's a list of predictions, isn't it? You wrote them down in German.'

'In case the list fell into the wrong hands,' said Faber. 'Which it did.'

Tig put her own list besides Faber's. Although she couldn't understand the language, it was clear that his list was longer.

'She's been telling you things when I'm not around, hasn't she?' said Tig. 'You have to tell me. What does this one say?'

'The carriage accident outside the theatre. The circle breaks, the chamber falls.'

'*Maschine*.' Tig pointed at another line. 'That must mean machine, right? Is this the one about—'

'Precious things behind and beneath the machines, yes. When you hurt your arms.'

'And Nelson cutting his hands?'

'This one,' said Faber. 'And this one –' he paused, swallowed hard, shook his head, 'this one says "follow the rabbit through the flames".'

'I heard that one too. I thought it was about the fire at the chemist.' Tig's stomach lurched. Now she thought about it, that one didn't quite make sense – she'd barely seen any flames in the fire, let alone gone through them. The floor seemed unsteady beneath her.

'No,' said Faber. 'I don't think that was it.'

Tig shivered violently. 'So that means . . . I'm going to be in the middle of the next fire? The one she just predicted?'

'It might not be about you,' said Faber.

'It says "rabbit".'

'It could mean an actual rabbit.'

'Oh yes, one of the many wild rabbits seen in the streets of Manchester! We're in the middle of a city, professor, of course it means me! And Euphonia said "Antigone".'

'I didn't want to frighten you.'

'It's not frightening me – it's warning me! If I'm going to be in a fire, don't I deserve a warning?'

'You are still not paying attention! Everything she said is coming true. It makes no difference if you have a warning or not. The fire will happen either way. At least this way I could spare you the worry.'

'What do these two say?' said Tig, pointing to another line that hadn't been crossed out.

'It means "the worker bees smoked from their hive".'

'"Worker bees"!' Tig's eyes widened. 'That's what they call the people of Manchester. All buzzing in and out of the factories.' She copied down the translations into her own notes. 'And smoke. So many of these predictions are about fire. Are they all about the same event?'

'I had considered as much.'

'Do you know what's going to happen?' Fire and smoke and flames and two hundred people... All the tragedies Euphonia had predicted so far were tiny compared with this.

He shook his head.

She pointed at the last surviving prediction, which was quite high on the list, surrounded by many scratched-out lines. 'What about this one?'

Faber reached over her and snatched the paper away. 'You don't need to know about that one. It has nothing to do with the others, I assure you.'

'Then why not tell me?'

'So many questions! All the time you bother me with your endless questioning!' He took a breath. 'I can't talk about this any more. I'm sorry. I need to be alone.'

He showed her out of the Green Room and closed the door firmly behind her. Her thoughts were scrambled by this sudden change of pace. Whatever that last prediction said, it must have frightened him. Why else would he abruptly refuse to help her, when the situation had never been more serious?

Nelson! He was her only hope – she'd have to find him and get him to help her figure out what to do. But she hadn't seen him since he offered to lock up last night. He hadn't even stopped by to say good morning, which was very unusual for him.

Something was wrong, she could feel it.

She checked the workshop and all the storerooms, each in turn. She went through the dress circle in case he was in

211

there scrubbing the floors, but there was no sign of him. The ticket booth was empty, as was the gallery. There would be no reason for him to be in the office, but perhaps Eliza had sent him on an errand of some description. She tapped on the office door.

'Enter,' Snell's voice came from within.

She opened the door but stayed where she was, not wanting to be any closer to him than she could help. 'Do you know where Nelson is?'

'Nelson is no longer employed at this establishment.' Snell turned the page in his newspaper, refusing to look at Tig.

'What do you mean?' said Tig.

'I let him go last night,' said Snell.

The words were like a punch to the stomach. 'Why?'

'There was too much dead weight around here. The Royale can't afford to keep paying unnecessary wages. It seems that you are too invaluable to lose, Miss Rabbit.' He sneered cruelly. 'So Master Nelson was let go instead.'

'You can't do that! You can't fire him to punish me!'

'I can, and I have.'

'But Nelson – he's got a family to support, and he's injured! He won't be able to get a labouring job until his hand is healed—'

'All the more reason to let him go,' said Snell, disappearing back behind his newspaper. 'He's no use to me if he can't work.'

'That's not fair. He got hurt here, working for you!' Tig could feel anger rising through her body.

'The tiles in the foyer need polishing. Since Master

Nelson is no longer here, you will have to pick up his duties in addition to your own. I want to see my reflection in them by this afternoon.'

Tig clenched her hands tight and took a deep breath. She didn't have time to argue with Snell. 'Yes, sir.'

29

Final Call

She didn't bother even to pretend to do as she was told. There was too much at stake. Leaving the theatre, she headed to the right and turned onto Market Street, but once she was in the thick of the crowd she doubled back towards Nelson's house.

Snell was lying. He couldn't have fired Nelson last night. He had left the building when the Peeler was still there, and didn't come back until very late, after Nelson had gone. She had no trouble believing Snell would do something so nasty, but her gut told her that wasn't what had happened. So where *was* Nelson?

There was no answer when she knocked at the door of his house. She peered in through the grimy window, but there was no sign of anyone inside.

'Mornin', Miss Rabbit!' It was the little girl who sold fruit outside the theatre. She was emerging from a nearby ginnel, pushing a small barrow which was already loaded with her wares for the day.

'You're out early, miss.' The girl had a big smile and Tig noticed how white her apron was, even though the street was very dirty.

'I was looking for Nelson. He lives here. About my size, dark curly hair.'

'Yeah, I know Nelson. But I 'aven't seen him since yesterday morning.'

'Oh, that's a pity. Do you know where the rest of the family are?'

'The old woman, Ma Nelson, she'll already be out, I reckon. She takes in washing and ironing. The fella, what's 'is name? Lumpy. He'll be home any minute, I should think. He does nights at the factory.'

'Thanks,' said Tig. 'You've been a big help.'

She watched the girl push the barrow along the uneven cobbles out towards the market. She wondered what time they had to get up in the morning to go and get all the fruit ready for selling. She wondered where the oranges came from.

If Nelson's uncle was due back soon, she might as well wait for him. She hoped he wasn't long. Anxiously, she checked the list of predictions again. *The day is here.* Time was running out to work out what it meant.

Lumpy appeared around the corner not long afterwards.

'Hullo, Tig,' he said. 'You waiting for Nelson?'

'Didn't he tell you?'

'Tell me what?'

'He—' She stopped herself. Maybe Nelson didn't want to worry his family by letting them know he'd lost his job. That was just like him. Never a complaint. He always did his best and did it with a smile. 'Nothing. I've knocked but he doesn't seem to be home.'

'He wasn't home when I left for work last night,' said Lumpy. 'Late closing time at the theatre, I suppose? He must have gone in early, too. He's a hard worker, our Nelson!'

Did that mean . . . had Nelson not come home last night?

'Yes, he is,' said Tig. 'Well, I'll head back to the theatre and catch up with him there.'

Lumpy nodded and let himself in, ducking his head under the low doorframe.

There had to be a reasonable explanation. Nelson wasn't the type to run away or do anything silly. He probably got home late, and then got up early because he was looking for work. That was all.

But Tig just knew that it was something worse.

Nervously, she fished the paper out of her pocket and unfolded it. She scanned through the lines of predictions, but there didn't seem to be anything about Nelson or someone not coming home. Would Euphonia have warned her if Nelson was going to go missing? She always predicted bad things, but that didn't mean she would predict *every* bad thing. She hadn't predicted Snell stealing Professor Faber's plans after all.

When she returned to the theatre, Faber was standing

outside bare-headed and in his shirt sleeves. He was on the opposite side of the road to the theatre, pacing anxiously, ducking back and forth to avoid the people walking past.

'What's going on?' said Tig.

'Gas leak! A tiny spark could—' He clapped his hands then flung them wide, miming an explosion.

A jolt of panic. Theatres burned down all the time – they were notorious for it. Was this it? Was this what Euphonia was predicting? 'Is everyone out?'

'Yes. Yes. I believe so. Yes.' He folded his arms, then unfolded them, then clasped his hands behind his back. He was scared. 'The surly boy went that way.' He pointed up York Street, towards the train station and the hospital. 'And Eliza is there.'

Eliza was on the corner, also without a hat, talking to a lady outside the post office. Snell stood on the stone steps of the Royale's grand entrance speaking with a short man in builder's overalls. They both kept looking up at the building and gesturing towards it, though Tig couldn't hear what they were saying over the hubbub of the busy street.

'Who's that?'

'He came to fix the leak,' said Faber.

She noticed his hands were shaking slightly and knew he must be thinking about Euphonia's words. 'Do you think . . . is this the calamity she predicted? Even though it's not during a performance with hundreds of people inside?'

Faber didn't answer. He seemed lost in thought.

'It's all right now!' Snell shouted over the noise of the

217

horses and foot traffic. 'Everyone can go back inside!'

Faber strode across the road without looking.

A street sweeper almost tripped over him. 'Oi! Watch it, mate!'

'Sorry!' said Tig on Faber's behalf as she hurried after him.

He marched up the stairs. Snell and the short man had been joined by two others in similar clothing, who had emerged from the theatre. The older man wiped his hands on his overalls. 'False alarm, sir.'

'You're quite sure it's safe?' said Faber.

'I'd let me own grandmother go inside,' said the short man.

Faber nodded, puffed out his chest as if bracing himself for something, and entered the building.

'Why did you think there was a leak?' said Tig to Snell. 'What made you call them in?'

Snell glared at her. 'Get out of here. Shoo!'

Tig trudged up the stairs as slowly as she could, trying to catch a little more of the conversation. She couldn't think why Snell would lie about something like this, especially if it cost him money to have the gas men come and check it out, but lately she found everything he did suspicious.

When she reached the backstage area, the Green Room door was open. She stepped inside to see Faber, white-faced and wide-eyed, staring at the empty space by the wall where Euphoria should have been.

'She's been taken.' Faber sounded as though he could barely believe his own words.

'It had to be Snell,' whispered Tig. 'He invented the

gas leak because he knew you wouldn't leave the theatre willingly.'

'He was outside the whole time . . .' said Faber. 'He must have had someone helping him.'

'How long were you outside altogether?'

Faber consulted his pocket watch. 'Twenty minutes.'

'So, plenty of time to steal Euphonia,' said Tig. 'But suspiciously quick for the gas fitters to arrive and check all over this big building.'

'Perhaps whoever Snell sold the plans to realized it was too complicated to build, so they decided just to take her for themselves.' Faber sighed.

'Why didn't Euphonia warn us?' said Tig.

'It wouldn't have mattered,' answered Faber. 'The predictions can—'

'Never be prevented, I know.' She glanced at the clock and was struck by an idea. Tig scrabbled for her list of predictions.

'She did predict it! "A quarter to nine precisely the theatre thief will strike." I thought it meant quarter to nine at night, when the pickpocket was working, but actually it was this morning. The theft of the machine. Of her!'

It all fell into place.

Tig felt sick. For the first time since she arrived here, the Royale didn't feel safe. First Snell had tried to sell the theatre, and then, when he found out about what Euphonia could do, he had found another way to make his money.

Every nerve in her body was screaming. The whole time Euphonia's words 'the day is here' echoed in her head. She needed Nelson here to keep her calm.

'Nelson is missing,' said Tig. 'Snell said he fired him, but I've checked his house and he never went home.'

'Did he run away?'

'No,' said Tig. 'Nelson would never do that. He loves his family too much.'

She stared at the list of predictions. The answers were here. Euphonia had been trying to warn them.

'*Both precious things!*' She grabbed Faber's arm. 'My friend, and your machine. Our most precious things. They're both missing. It has to be connected! *Held captive below and behind and within the machines.* The prediction wasn't about me getting hurt in the stage machinery.'

Faber sank down into a chair.

'Professor, we got it all wrong. All of these predictions – I think they might all be about the same thing. The rescuer – Euphonia knew I'd try to rescue Nelson if he was captured, and that's when the fire is going to start.'

'You must not try anything of the sort,' said Faber. 'You've both already been hurt and Euphonia is gone. Isn't that bad enough?'

Tig's mind was working faster than it ever had before, and all the fear and panic were crystallizing into pure and shining hope.

'*Behind and beneath and within the machines* – they've hidden your machine somewhere with lots of other machines? Most of the machines round here are ... the worker bees! The hive of the worker bees – it has to be the mills! There's hundreds of workers in the mill . . . smoked out . . . We need to go. We need to find Nelson and Euphonia and stop the fire.'

'I can't.'

'We have to try! We're the only people in the whole world who have a chance! No matter how small. We have to take it!' She grabbed his sleeve. 'I'm just a child. My chances of finding Nelson and Euphonia and saving everyone are so much better if you help me. Please!'

'No.'

'Why? Why won't you try?' Despair and fury and frustration crashed in great waves over her.

'The other prediction. The one I didn't translate for you.' His eyes were unfocused, and his voice was almost drowned out by the roaring of blood through Tig's veins.

Tig fell silent, seeing the fear on Faber's face.

'It said that I am going to die here in Manchester.' He dropped his head and covered his eyes with his hand. 'And Euphonia is—'

'Never wrong.' A million thoughts flooded Tig's brain, vying for her attention. All this bother about health tonics and malaria and chimney fumes – all this time he had been expecting his own death, wondering what was going to kill him. It was as though the world slowed down for a moment, and in the gaps between heartbeats Tig felt a rush of sympathy for him. Imagine knowing with absolute certainly that death was on its way, and that you could do nothing to prevent it.

'She's never wrong,' Faber repeated.

'We don't know for certain,' said Tig.

221

'She told me the first night I was here. It didn't scare me much at first, but then one by one every other prediction has come true.'

'Well then,' said Tig. 'If you're so certain that you're going to die today, you might as well help me. Wouldn't you rather die a hero than a coward?'

He opened his mouth and paused on the verge of speaking.

'Please,' said Tig.

'I can't.'

30

Rising Action

Tig left Faber behind. Perhaps he was right, and they were doomed either way. But if she was going to lose, then she'd rather go down fighting.

Nelson was being kept in a mill, with Euphonia, she was sure of it. Euphonia had disappeared from the theatre in less than twenty minutes, and Faber would have spotted it if they carried the machine down Spring Gardens. So the thieves must have used the back entrance.

The most logical place for it, then, was the mill directly behind the Royale. They could easily have carried Euphonia out of the stage doors and into the mill in a matter of minutes. That's what she hoped, anyway. Not to mention the fact that nasty Mr Albion was a friend of Snell's, and wanted to buy the building. Of course it would be in his mill.

Despite living next door to one, Tig had never been inside a cotton mill before.

Getting in was easy enough. She simply joined the line of girls making their way back into the building after their dinner break, and kept her head down so no one would notice that she didn't belong there. She needn't have worried – the mill was so full of people, most of them around Tig's age – that she blended right into the crowd.

As they passed through the doorway she noticed a bee carved into the stonework above. This was the right place – the *worker bees*. Euphonia had said *beneath and behind the machinery*, so she would start her search on the lowest floor, where the loading bays were. The mill was built on a slope, so that the employees entered on the floor above.

It was uncomfortably hot inside the mill. Her skin felt damp very quickly. Cotton grew in hot, damp places in the colonies, and would get soon dried out and brittle in the cold. It was also extremely noisy. On the main floor she was greeted by rows and rows of weaving machines, each one reaching from floor to ceiling, great mechanical monstrosities which roared and clattered like a thousand horse-drawn carriages at once. Metallic beams swung backwards and forwards at great speed, shuttles slammed from side to side, reels spun round releasing cotton thread, and wheels on the ceiling spun, driving the belts that made the whole machine work.

Between and beside and beneath these machines children worked, darting from one loom to the next, occasionally stopping to refill a bobbin or prise apart a piece that had jammed. Some of the children were no more than eight or nine, skinny, pale, underfed little things. Tig tried to get the attention of a little boy with a broom.

'Which way is the loading bay?'

The boy pointed to his ear and shrugged – he couldn't hear her over the din.

'Where do you take the cloth when it's finished?' she tried again, but he glanced over her shoulder and suddenly dashed off round the other side of his machine. Tig looked behind her – an older lady was pacing between the rows, keeping an eye on the children. Tig took the boy's lead and stepped between two looms, out of sight. She must be some sort of supervisor, and Tig didn't want to explain what she was doing in here.

She waited until the supervisor was out of sight before slipping through a large blue door. She found herself in a brick-lined stairwell. It was completely empty of people.

She took a deep breath and held her head high. She had to keep her nerve. Somewhere, Nelson was counting on her. If she couldn't rescue him, at least she'd know she tried.

The noise of the machinery muffled the sound of Tig's

footsteps as she descended. It was so loud, the brick walls only serving to echo and amplify the rattling. She couldn't imagine having to work in this heat and noise for twelve hours a day.

At the bottom of the stairs she came into a long, narrow warehouse, with wooden crates covered by sheets standing in neat rows. She peered around the corner of one. Right down at the end, two men were sitting on boxes eating sandwiches. She veered the other way. On her left, the large arched double doors led through to the street. On the right were four smaller doors.

Creeping towards the first one, she opened it just a crack, peering through. She couldn't make out what was inside – big stacks . . . no, bales of cotton. This must be where they stored it when it first arrived. But she couldn't see how far the room continued beyond the bales, or whether anything else might be hidden at the other end. Her heart sank. She'd have to search every inch of the place. And if she found Euphonia and Nelson, then what?

The sort of person who would kidnap Nelson probably couldn't be reasoned with. She could hardly fight her way out, and there was no hope of retrieving the machine on her own.

But then she heard a noise. Almost inaudible over the drone of looms on the floor above, but unmistakably different.

Euphonia's voice.

Tig moved further along the wall, listening hard. She crept to the third door along, labelled 'Carding', and pressed her ear up against the wood.

Yes, that was Euphonia for sure, but her voice was garbled, strings of nonsense sounds. She wasn't making a prediction – someone was trying to play her. Someone who didn't understand how she worked.

Tig hesitated with her hand on the door handle. Perhaps she should go back and once again ask Faber to help her – perhaps they could raise the Peelers and report that the mill was hiding stolen goods.

A hand landed on her shoulder.

31

Exeunt

'Tig Rabbit. Never could mind your own business, could you?'

'Gus? What are you doing here? Get off me!' She shrugged his hand away but he caught her wrists instead.

'Mr Snell asked for my help. Should've known you'd turn up and get in the way.'

'Where's Nelson?' she demanded. 'If someone has hurt him, I swear—'

'Shut up, Tig.'

'You stole the plans for Snell, didn't you? I knew it had to be someone in the theatre.'

'Maybe,' he said. 'None of your business.'

'Why are you helping Snell? He's a horrible, horrible man!' She twisted around, trying to yank her wrists free, but Gus held tight.

'You're jealous because he likes me. He's going to make me deputy theatre manager once all this is done.'

'He's lying to you! There won't even *be* a theatre to manage. That's what all of this is about – he's selling the theatre to Mr Albion.'

'You're the one who's lying,' Gus said, but there was a flicker of doubt in his eyes. 'He promised.'

'He doesn't care about you.' She still hoped to persuade him to help her, but she was ready to kick him in the shins if she needed to. 'He's got you stealing for him – you could get in real trouble!'

'It felt wrong, taking the whole machine,' he admitted. 'But Mr Snell said we had no choice. Him and Mr Albion – they're a bit scary.'

'Yes!' Tig nodded furiously. 'You can't trust them.'

'I don't trust you either, Rabbit. You just don't want me to get my promotion.'

There wasn't time to explain all the ways that Snell was manipulating him. Nelson was in danger. They were all in danger. She changed strategy. 'Fine. Don't believe me. But there's going to be a fire – the machine told me. Please. Let's get Nelson and go.' She could see he was softening. 'I don't know how long we've got. Come on. Help me.'

He let go of her left hand.

'Yes! Thank you, let's go!'

'Mr Snell!' Gus bellowed. 'Rabbit's here!'

He opened the door and shoved her through it. She almost lost her balance on the rough stone slabs but caught herself. 'Mr Snell!'

There were several machines in this room, though none of them seemed to be currently working. Unlike the looms upstairs, these resembled huge barrels laid on their side, or the wheel of a water-mill, with nine or ten smaller rollers stuck to it all around. Fluffy white cotton coated the rollers like hair caught in a hairbrush, and the air was thick with cotton dust that made Tig's throat itch.

'Come on, Gus. Don't be stupid. We've got to get to safety.'

'I'll show you where Nelson is.' He grabbed her by the elbow and marched her down between the machines. She pulled away from him with all her might but he was older and stronger.

Snell appeared round the corner.

'She was snooping around, Mr Snell,' said Gus.

'Of course she was,' said Snell. 'Good work, son.'

Gus made a smug, told-you-so face as he handed her over to Snell, who took her by the forearm and started walking.

'I never liked you,' said Snell.

'Oh, really?' said Tig. 'I thought we were friends.'

'Shut up.' He coughed. 'Wretched child. Always sticking your nose where it doesn't belong. I told Eliza not to take you in, silly woman, it was only because she felt guilty about Antigone.'

'What do you mean, Antigo—'

'Shut up, brat. Since you're here –' he turned sharply behind the last machine to where an open archway led into a side room, 'you can make yourself useful.'

He gave her another shove and this time she did fall, tripping down the two steps onto the lower level and landing with a stinging slap on the floor.

'Tig!'

Nelson was in the corner of the room, sitting with his back against the wall. His eyes were puffy – it looked like he had been crying.

'Nelson, what happened? Did they hurt you?' She scurried across the floor towards him.

'No, I'm fine. He grabbed me outside the theatre last night after I locked up.' He pointed to Albion. 'They think I can make Euphonia talk. He says Gus saw me.'

Euphonia stood in the opposite corner. Her rubber face had been peeled back, and lay on the grubby floor with the tangled wig. Obviously they had been trying to figure out how she worked. Behind Euphonia was Albion, standing in a menacing posture with folded arms and a glowering stare.

An oil lamp sat on the flat tabletop section by the keys. It would leave a mark on the polished wood. Faber would be furious.

Snell brushed some cotton fluff off his black jacket sleeves. 'This is the girl that's always skulking about with Faber.'

'Give the professor his machine back,' said Tig. 'And let Nelson go.'

'Make it talk,' said the man.

'No,' said Tig.

'Show some manners,' said Snell. 'Mr Albion is the owner of this fine mill. Soon to be owner of the Royale, too.'

Gus flinched at this. Tig almost felt sorry for him.

'Well, Mr Snell? Get her to make it talk!' Albion yelled.

Snell strode over to where Nelson sat and pulled him up by his ear. 'Make it talk.'

'Let go of him first, and I'll do it,' said Tig.

Snell and Albion exchanged looks, but after a moment Snell released Nelson.

Tig approached Euphonia. She stroked the mechanical skull and murmured, 'It's me, Tig.'

She placed her hands on the keys. There was no stool to sit at, which made the angle awkward, but she put her foot on the bellows and pressed down firmly. Euphonia made a humming sound. Tig eased down the lever which opened the throat and allowed the air to pass through fully. The hum opened out into an 'ahhh' sound.

She wished she knew how to operate the machinery. She had seen Faber do this many times, but still didn't understand how he knew what keys he needed to press to form a word. The one furthest to the left made Euphonia clamp her lips closed, and open them once it was released. Euphonia made a sound which was a bit like 'mama'.

'Not like that,' said Snell. 'Make it tell the future.'

'I don't know what you mean,' said Tig. He thought he was so clever. Selling the machine would make him extra money, and guarantee Faber's show would fail and the theatre would close.

'Oh yes?' said Albion. 'Then how come your snivelly little friend was bragging down in the Three Arrows about how

232

it predicted him getting his hand cut open?'

'It was a story, right, Nelson?'

'Right, just a story!' Nelson nodded.

'I don't believe you,' said Snell. 'And Mr Albion here has paid good money for this thing. So you'd better make it work.'

'The dogs,' said Albion. 'Make it tell me which dog to bet on tonight.'

'It doesn't work like that,' said Nelson.

'She only speaks when she wants to,' said Tig. 'And she usually predicts bad things. Accidents.'

'I've paid for a machine that talks, so make it talk!' said Albion. He was scary in a different way to Snell. Where Snell liked to use his power to make them miserable, Albion seemed like someone who solved most of his problems with his fists.

'I can't,' said Tig.

'I don't want to hurt you,' said Snell.

Albion crossed the floor, opened a chest and pulled out a hatchet. 'I have no issues with hurting you. Show me how to make it work or you'll be sorry.'

Even Snell went pale at this. 'Come now, Albion, there's no need for that.'

'I can't control her,' Tig insisted.

Albion snarled, his knuckles white around the hatchet handle.

'Let Nelson leave.'

'Absolutely not,' said Snell.

'And Gus. Let them go.'

'I'm losing my patience!' growled Albion.

Tig kept her eyes on Snell. There had to be some scrap of reason in him that she could reach. 'Faber knows it was you,' said Tig. 'He'll go to the Peelers.'

'Liar,' said Snell. 'If Faber knows, then where is he? Hmm? Why did he send his maid to fight his battles for him?'

'We need to leave,' said Tig. 'Euphonia predicted there's going to be a fire. An awful one. And all her predictions have come true so far. They've been leading up to this. We're all in danger.' Tig looked to Albion. 'Your workers are in danger.'

'Nice try,' said Albion. 'You're not going anywhere until the machine starts speaking.'

Tig leaned close to Euphonia's face and whispered, 'Please tell them. Tell them it isn't safe here.' Perhaps it was impossible for Euphonia to speak here, outside the walls of the Royale. It was Cold Annie who made the machine work, and Tig had no way of knowing whether Annie could leave the theatre. 'Or tell me what to do. I don't know what to do.'

'It doesn't work, Snell. You've got no proof. These children know nothing. You've cheated me,' Albion accused him. 'I want my money back.'

'Absolutely not!' said Snell. 'Our agreement was that I would get you the machine. It's not my fault if you can't work it.'

'No?' Albion was getting louder and louder. 'I'll show you what I think of your machine.'

Albion grabbed Tig by the shoulder of her dress and threw her aside. He pulled back the hatchet and brought it down, CRACK, on Euphonia's wooden surface. He swung

234

it back, and hit it a second time. CRACK.

On the third strike, the blade slipped. It skimmed over the corner of Euphonia, splintering off a chunk of the wood, which flew through the air and crashed right through the fragile glass tube of the oil lamp.

It happened so fast. The flame and the spilled oil touched the cotton fluff floating everywhere, and it caught fire. Tig screamed and instinctively fell to the ground as a hot wave tore through the air. For a moment she was blinded with the light of it.

'My mill!' shouted Albion to Snell. 'You'll pay for this!'

Tig gasped as she was roughly pushed aside by Albion. He raced from the room, between the carding machines and straight out of the door. Snell turned to Tig, shock and anger etched into his face, but he said nothing, just turned and fled.

Tig ran to Nelson and flung her arms around him. 'I'm so glad you're safe!'

Nelson squeezed her back. 'Don't worry. I was about to escape!'

They smiled at each other briefly before glancing behind them, where the fire was growing and starting to race up the walls, fuelled by a million tiny scraps of cotton in the air and in every crevice of the brickwork. Cotton was so flammable. The whole place would go up in smoke in minutes.

'Gus! Come on!' she shouted.

They ran from the room and saw Albion fumble with the keys by the door of the loading bay.

'Unlock it! Quick!' Snell hopped frantically from foot

to foot, glancing back over his shoulder to see the flames creeping through the carding room towards them.

'Where are you going?' shouted Tig. 'Your workers! The fire!'

The door opened and Snell and Albion tumbled through them to the safety of the street beyond.

Wait.

That was one of Euphonia's predictions – *so much fuel, black smoke, your friend must run.*

Two hundred souls. There were two hundred people in this burning building.

Your friend must run.

'Run to the fire station,' Tig said to Nelson. 'Raise the alarm. I need to warn the workers.'

Nelson nodded. 'Be careful.'

'What about me?' said Gus.

'I don't care,' said Tig. 'Just try not to die!'

'I'm coming with you.'

She ran through the warehouse towards the stairs and Gus followed behind. The looms above still hammered out their steady rhythm, completely unaware of the danger.

'We'll be quicker if we split up!'

Gus's shout was almost swallowed up by roaring machinery but Tig understood. They emerged, breathless, into the weaving room.

'Fire!' she shouted at the top of her lungs, but no one could hear her.

Gus ran down the nearest row, tapping the shoulders of the weavers. Tig took the next row and grabbed the little boy who was piecing cotton thread. She pulled him close and shouted into his ear. 'Fire! Everybody out! Run!'

The little boy's eyes went wide and he turned tail and raced down towards the doors, waving his arms frantically over his head. The woman a few machines down saw him, and within a moment, she too was running. Tig darted to the next row. 'Fire! Fire!'

She left them to spread the message as she returned to the stairs and ran up. As she reached the top there was a groan and the clattering noise dimmed, voices rising up in its place. Good. Someone had turned off the engine that drove the machines, and people were shouting to each other to get out.

On the next floor she repeated the process, grabbing the nearest worker, a stout woman of middle age, and screaming into her ear. The woman ran off, flapping her hands to the other women and girls on the row.

Tig went up to the top floor, breathless and hot. Perhaps it was the exertion, or perhaps the fire was already catching up with her. Gus met her on the stairs, his longer legs overtaking her. This top floor was lace makers – no heavy machinery here, just a group of some twenty or so women with their heads down over their delicate needlework.

'Fire!' Tig gasped.

The women looked up, startled.

'There's a fire in the warehouse. You need to get out now. Run! Please!'

'This way, follow me,' shouted Gus, and led the charge back down.

A surge of women came towards her, jostling each other as they pushed through the narrow opening and flooded down the stairs, mixing with the last of the people on the floor below. With the loading bay now well and truly ablaze, the only way out was back through the weaving floor of the mill. It was filling up already with black smoke – the worker bees were being smoked out of their hive. Tig pulled the collar of her dress up over her mouth and nose. It was hard going through the centre of the mill, with so many things to trip over and lots of noise, but at last she was out.

From the street she could see that the fire was spreading incredibly fast. Flames billowed out of the windows of the staircase where she had been standing only moments before.

Smoke and people poured out of the building, and a bubble of empty space had formed around the mill as carriages held back their horses and pedestrians watched from the other side of the street. Tig had done all she could. She only hoped everyone had got out in time. And where was Gus? He was a traitorous little worm but he had, in the end, been very brave, and she couldn't stand to see him harmed.

She rounded the building, dodging through the gathering crowd to get back home. She had to warn Eliza, and find Faber.

As she passed the edge of the building, through the narrow ginnel between the back of the mill and the back of the theatre, she saw her worst fears confirmed. The flames had crossed the gap.

The Royale was burning.

32

Set Piece

The back door of the workshop was no longer accessible. Tig raced round to the front of the building and saw with some relief that Gus was there, a little way ahead of her.

'Gus! The theatre's on fire!' she shouted. 'You get Eliza out. I'm going for the professor.'

He dashed up the stairs and into the lobby. 'Fire! Mrs Lincoln, fire!'

Tig entered the lobby as Eliza and Gus were on their way out.

'The whole back wall is on fire,' Tig panted. 'I'm going for Faber.'

Eliza snatched her dress and held her back. 'No, Tig, it's too dangerous!'

'I have to! The back door is covered with flames. Faber will never be able to find his way through all the stagehands' passages in the dark and smoke.'

'Tig!' Eliza's looked terrified but Tig pulled herself away and started running.

Euphonia said Faber was going to die. Was this how it happened? Maybe she should turn back, and save herself. But her legs kept pushing her onwards. She entered the auditorium and raced down the centre aisle. Smoke was coming through here too, drawn upwards into the dome in the ceiling.

She hoisted herself up onto the stage. 'Professor Faber!' she shouted.

He wasn't a bad man, not really. When she left him earlier, she had been so sure she would never help him again. His cowardice was unforgiveable. But now, thinking of him all alone in the burning theatre, she saw him differently. Not bad. Just scared and lonely.

Tig let out a scream of frustration and looked up into the cavernous flies above the stage.

Up there, beyond the rising smoke, stood the bluish shape of Cold Annie. The ghost walked along the beam towards the Green Room and vanished.

Tig ran to the side of the stage where the Green Room was, but the exit was inaccessible. The backdrop cloth was burning, the fire eating away at the fabric until it hung in flaming rags, blocking her path.

She couldn't bring him out that way. She looked up to where Annie had stood moments earlier. There was only one other route into Faber's rooms.

At the opposite side of the stage, she climbed the metal ladder up to the beams in the flies. She had to move fast, for now the smoke was being pulled up high above her head.

She ducked through the railings and out onto the same girder she had almost fallen from the day Faber arrived. She crawled across the beam on hands and knees. 'Professor Faber! Come up! Up the ladder! You have to come up!'

Nothing. He mustn't be able to hear her over the flames! Or was he . . . no. It was the noise. Had to be the noise.

Fire was loud. Surprisingly loud. Tig reached the end of the beam and stepped lightly across the catwalk. She grabbed the top of the ladder and descended a few steps down into the Green Room. And there he was, huddled in the corner, his knees to his chest. His bedclothes had been stuffed under the door, perhaps to keep the smoke out.

'Professor!'

He looked up, and a mixture of relief and shock covered his face.

'You came back for me.'

'Come on! Up the ladder!'

'I can't go up there. I'll fall.'

'There's no other choice,' she said. 'Come on.'

She held out her hand and Faber took it, getting shakily to his feet. Tig guided him to the ladder, 'You go first!'

Her heart was beating harder than it ever had before, but the fear was dull and distant – for once her mind was clear and calm. She knew what to do. She was going to get Faber to safety.

At the top Tig could see the smoke had got thicker. They needed to get out, fast. 'We have to go across,' she shouted to him. 'It's the only way down.'

Faber didn't say anything. She pushed him gently towards the beam.

'You can do it. It's wide enough to crawl along. Keep your eyes on the end of the beam and just keep moving.'

He nodded.

'Go!'

He lowered himself unsteadily to his knees and cautiously put one hand out onto the beam, as if he didn't know whether it would hold his weight.

They inched across, one agonizing second at a time, the girder growing warm beneath their hands. 'Keep going, keep going, nearly there,' Tig kept repeating, though she wasn't sure if he could hear her.

The roof had caught fire now. One of the wooden bars that held the coloured mediums over the gaslights cracked and fell to the stage like a flaming torch. Tig glanced out over the auditorium – it was filled with yellow light and odd shadows as the flames felt their way around the building. Her precious Royale. Gone.

She pulled the collar of her dress up over her mouth and nose but she could still taste the smoke, gritty and hot and bitter.

An eternity later Faber reached the other end.

'That's it, there's a ladder under the railing,' said Tig. 'Just turn yourself around and feel for the rungs with your feet.'

Faber turned, and as he did so he looked down. He almost swooned, fear painted all over his face, but he caught himself, and down he went. Tig hurried after him, jumping the last four rungs down to the floor.

How long had they been inside, now? How much longer did they have?

'We'll jump down and go up through the seats!' she shouted, but before they reached the edge of the stage there was an unearthly crash. The front edge of the dress circle had collapsed, showering the first few rows with brick and plaster. They couldn't risk going beneath it in case the whole thing tumbled down. Another exit was blocked. The fall caused a chain reaction and the topmost royal box crumbled, dropping chairs through to the lower level.

The circle breaks. The chamber falls.

She grabbed Faber by the hand. 'Follow me. And don't let go.'

Darting behind the red velvet curtains, she pushed open the narrow door and shoved through into the stagehands' short cut.

'Eight steps,' she said. 'Keep your head low.'

The passageway was so narrow, completely dark and suffocatingly hot. It wasn't really big enough for an adult. It was lucky that Faber was so thin. If they got stuck . . .

Thin tendrils of smoke followed them into the space and stung Tig's eyes and throat. She fumbled to find the catch with one hand and then – relief – the door swung open.

'We've done it,' said Tig, suddenly fighting back tears.

'We're going to be fine. Just keep going.'

Ahead of them again, as though urging them on, was Annie's shape, the only light in the darkness. But at the end of the corridor, instead of going into the lobby, the ghost turned sharply and vanished into the Minshull Gallery.

Tig sent her silent thanks to the ghost and then led Faber along the corridor, her legs remembering where to hop down the steps that she couldn't see. Faber was right behind her, stumbling, but still following. They rounded the corner and spilled out through the stalls doors into the beautiful, cool, clean air of the foyer.

In sheer relief she threw her arms around Faber's neck, and after a moment's hesitation, he hugged her back.

As they came down the steps, Eliza rushed over to meet them. Someone had given her a red shawl to cover her bare shoulders and it flapped behind her like a warning flag as she ran.

The widow wears red.

'Where's Nelson?' she said. 'He went back in to shut off the gas supply. You didn't see him?'

Tig shook her head.

'He's been in there too long,' said Eliza. 'It shouldn't take that long to reach the stopcock.'

The stopcock. Of course! If the fire reached the gas lines, there would be a huge explosion. On a busy city street, that could mean untold numbers of casualties. Nelson had put himself in danger to keep everyone else safe.

The stopcock was downstairs by Eliza's apartment. Down

the stairs in the Minshull Gallery – that must have been why Annie headed that way.

'I'm going back for him,' said Tig.

'You can't.' Eliza held Tig's wrist tight. 'The fire is out of control now.'

'I can't just leave him in there!' Tears started to spill down Tig's face and she wiped them away angrily. She didn't have time for tears.

'I'll go,' said Faber. He took off his jacket and handed it to Tig.

'But Euphonia said—'

He rolled up his sleeves. His face was grim, but his eyes were blazing. 'You came back for me. You did the right thing. Now it's my turn.'

'Euphonia said you'd die,' said Tig. 'She didn't say that about me. Maybe if I go...'

'What was it you said? If I'm going to die, better to die as a hero.' He took out his handkerchief and began tying it round his face as a makeshift mask. 'Where is it?'

'Through the lobby,' said Eliza, wrapping her arms around Tig's heaving shoulders, both comforting her and holding her back. 'Turn right into the Minshull Gallery. Straight down the stairs.'

Faber nodded. 'Get everybody further back in case it...' He paused, closed his eyes for a second, and took a deep breath. 'In case it explodes.'

Faber ran up the steps and back into the Royale.

33

The Tragic Hero

Tig waited with Eliza halfway down the street, just in sight of the front steps of the Royale. Mill workers, street sweepers and afternoon shoppers alike craned their necks to get a view of the fire. Tig rested her head on Eliza's shoulder as they both watched their whole world burn.

Nelson. He'd suffered so much, and none of it was his fault. And Professor Faber – frustrating, grumpy, unpleasant Faber, who had refused and refused to try and stop Euphonia's predictions – had in the end stepped up and done the right thing.

Everything happened exactly as Euphonia had said it would. She must be ashes by now. Had she known she was going to burn?

Hearing a shout, Tig looked up.

The doors of the Royale had opened. Smoke pooled

out and the shape of a man emerged from the fog. Faber staggered, but Tig saw that he was holding something in his arms. Nelson.

She ran full pelt towards them. Men from the crowd came forward too, and met Faber halfway up the stairs, lifting Nelson out of his arms. Faber leaned heavily against the pillars, wheezing, and then slumped over entirely and collapsed, sprawled out on the stone steps.

'Move them!' shouted Tig. 'Get them away from the building.'

'I've got him,' said a burly man in worker's cords, taking up Nelson and cradling him as though he were no more than a baby.

'Take them both over to my shop,' said Mr Becker, running towards them. 'The chemist. Matilde! Matilde, go for Doctor Ball!'

'I did it,' came a little voice from Nelson. 'The gas . . . I turned it off.' He coughed and Tig could finally breathe.

'All right, good lad, no talking now,' said the man who was carrying him. 'Let's get you safe.'

She turned to Faber who wasn't stirring at all.

'Mind out, love,' said a man. He put his hands under Faber's armpits and another man picked up his feet. They lifted him together, his head lolling back.

'Is he dead?' said Tig, but nobody was paying any attention to her.

She swallowed hard and followed them to the chemist shop.

Tig tugged at Mr Becker's sleeve. 'Is the professor . . .' her voice cracked. 'Is he dead?'

'Heavens, no, child. Hurry now, we need to help them.'

Nelson and Faber were laid down to recover in the cool quiet of Mr Becker's parlour, where Tig had never been allowed before. Nelson was propped up in a chair with his feet on a stool, and was soon alert and talking.

'Hush, boy. Drink this.' Mr Becker presented him with a small glass of something that looked like tar.

'Ick.' Nelson screwed up his face. 'What is it?'

'An expectorant,' said Becker. 'To help you cough up all that nasty soot in your lungs.'

'You were very brave,' said Eliza. She hadn't spoken except to fuss over Nelson like a mother hen. She hadn't said anything about the loss of her theatre, even though it was still burning not far away.

'Here you go,' said Matilde, handing Tig a cup.

'I'm not hurt,' she said. 'I don't need any medicine.'

'It's just strong tea,' said Matilde. 'For the shock.'

'Thank you.'

Mr Becker and Eliza retreated into the next room to talk in hushed, serious tones while Matilde went out front to serve a customer in the chemist shop.

'I'm sorry I got you hurt, again,' said Tig. 'I thought . . .' She blinked away a tear, hoping Nelson hadn't seen it. 'I thought you wouldn't make it out. Cold Annie tried to tell me you were in the basement but I was so desperate to escape . . .'

He reached out his good hand and squeezed hers.

249

'I didn't mean for any of this to happen.' She squeezed back.

'I know.'

'I wanted to do the right thing but everything got so muddled up, I didn't know what the right thing was any more.'

'Me neither,' said Nelson. 'But you got all those people out of the mill. Two hundred lives saved.'

'Or,' said Tig with a sigh. 'Perhaps they would never have been in danger, if not for me.'

'I'm sorry we couldn't save the theatre,' said Nelson, his voice crackly and hoarse. 'I wonder what will happen to us all now it's gone.'

'Right,' said Eliza from the doorway. 'Mr Becker has said that Nelson is well enough to go home, so I will walk you back myself. News of the fire will be everywhere soon, and I don't want your dear grandmother worrying about you.'

Nelson got to his feet.

'Can I come?' asked Tig.

'You stay here and rest, Miss Rabbit,' called Mr Becker from the next room. 'Sit with your professor in case he wakes and needs anything.'

'Wait a second,' she said. Jumping up from her seat she gathered Nelson into a big, long, hug which smelled of turpentine and wood smoke.

Faber didn't stir for hours, though Mr Becker didn't seem too concerned. Tig didn't leave his side – he had saved her best friend, so she owed him that at least. When night fell, Matilde left Tig with a candle and a book to read, but she found she couldn't concentrate on words.

'Where am I?' Faber sounded groggy.

'You're awake!' said Tig. 'Don't try to sit up. You need to rest.'

'What happened?'

'You went back for Nelson, do you remember?'

Faber coughed, and Tig rushed to give him some water, helping him hold the cup. 'Did I find him?'

'You did. You saved him.'

'And Euphonia?'

'I'm sorry,' said Tig. 'She's ... gone.'

Faber closed his eyes. 'My mouth tastes like charcoal.'

'The doctor says you're going to be fine.'

'What time is it?'

'Almost two in the morning,' said Tig. 'And you're not dead. We managed to stop Euphonia's prediction after all. We fought our fate,' she said. 'And maybe on this one thing, we won.'

The professor smiled and closed his eyes. 'Did we?' he said gently. 'Or did we do exactly what we were fated to do all along?'

34

Finale

'Everyone ready?'

Tig and Nelson sat on the stairs in the lobby, and Eliza stood beside them. The auditorium and the dressing rooms had been destroyed in the fire, but the lobby with all its marble and stone was still intact. For the last four weeks they'd spent most of their days here, salvaging what they could from the building, and meeting with insurance men, architects and reporters. Faber had even used the lobby as a workshop.

'Ready!' said Nelson.

'Ladies and gentlemen,' said Faber. 'Euphonia!'

He pulled off the cover with a showman's flourish to reveal the machine, and they all applauded.

The wooden frame and the bellows had been completely consumed in the fire, and the rubber valves had melted.

Once the embers of the mill were cool they had found the remains of her head and shoulders. She was tarnished, and a little dented, but with love and attention, Faber had returned her to her former glory. All except the face, of course, which had perished in the blaze. Faber said he would have to hire somebody to make a new one – it was a job for an artist, not an inventor.

As soon as the doctor declared him strong enough for work, he had dedicated all his hours to recreating the complex mechanisms that made her function. After spending all those years perfecting and obsessing over his creation, it turned out he was able to redraw most of his plans from memory.

'She looks even better than before,' said Tig.

'And so do you, professor,' said Eliza. 'You've even got some colour in your cheeks.'

'Ahem.' Faber pretended to be very interested in a smudge on the woodwork, but Tig could see he was blushing.

'You know,' said Eliza. 'I never really looked at her close up before.'

'Isn't she beautiful?' said Nelson.

'The eyes,' said Eliza. 'Why did you choose different-coloured eyes, professor?'

'They were both blue, but one of them broke,' he said.

'And Tig replaced it with the brown one,' added Nelson.

'However did you get hold of a glass eye, pet?'

'I found it under the stage. The ghost led me to it. Cold Annie. I think it must've been hers.'

Eliza stepped back suddenly. She clutched her chest and

looked like she might swoon. 'You found the eye? But ... we looked everywhere. Why didn't you tell me?'

'I was going to, but...' But Eliza had been cross and thought Tig was making up stories and causing trouble. That was over now, though, so instead Tig said, 'Did you know her? When she was alive?'

'Back when I first took over the Royale. There was an accident with the star trap. She was terribly hurt, poor thing, and her glass eye was lost.' Eliza took herself over to the steps and sat down. Her voice was a little choked as she continued. 'She died, a few days later, from her injuries. Those kinds of things ... that's how ghost stories start. I fancied I'd glimpsed her once or twice but I put that down to imagination.'

'Did she really know when things were going to go wrong, like they say?' asked Nelson, sitting at Eliza's feet.

'That's right ... they used to joke that the glass eye was magic – that it saw into the future.' Eliza laughed at the memory. 'I didn't really know her, the play had only been running for a week when the accident happened. But I'll never forget her.' She put her fingers to her temples and closed her eyes. 'Annie. Antigone Jones.'

Tig and Nelson gasped in one voice.

'You said—' Nelson jumped to his feet. 'You said you were named after an aunty!'

'And my mother had a relative in the theatre,' said Tig. 'I remember coming to see her when I was very small.'

'And the eye!' Nelson hopped up and down. 'I said it was just like yours, didn't I? Look Eliza, look.'

Eliza got up and looked again at Euphonia's face. She lifted Tig's chin.

'My goodness,' she said.

'You're not surprised, are you?' said Tig. 'You already knew we were related.'

'Your mother didn't want you to know. When she sent you here clutching that letter, saying you had nowhere else to go if I didn't find you a job, well ... it was like fate. A chance to make up for my part in the accident.'

'Your part?'

'My theatre. My show. My stage. People had been saying for years those traps were dangerous...'

'And that's why you stopped Snell from firing me so many times.'

A moment of stillness fell over the Royale as each of them considered this revelation.

Snell. The name tasted rotten in Tig's mouth.

'Well then,' said Faber at last. 'I believe my time here has finished. I can't thank you enough for your kindness. I hope Mr Snell doesn't cause you any more bother.'

'No need to worry about my brother,' said Eliza. 'Useless lump won't dare show his face around here any more.'

He had been back to the theatre exactly once to collect what was left of his belongings after the fire. Eliza had helped him by throwing it all down the front stairs and onto the filthy street, while giving him a piece of her mind. Lawyers had been involved, and certain papers signed that gave Eliza full control of the Royale, in exchange for not informing the police of the thieving and kidnapping he had been party to. Gus was gone, too. He was ashamed of his part in the whole affair, and didn't want to return – Eliza had called in a favour and got him an apprenticeship at the piano makers down on Deansgate.

'And your beautiful theatre, I'm so sorry.'

'Ah well,' said Eliza. 'My brother did do one good thing for me. Fire insurance. If I'd known how much it was worth I'd have burned the place down years ago.'

Tig must have look horrified at this, because Eliza added, 'I'm kidding, Tig!'

'I'm sure the new building will be excellent,' said Faber.

'Must you really go?' Tig asked.

'Of course he must, pet,' said Eliza. 'He can't sit around and wait for us to reopen.'

'I hope I'm not out of line for asking, but Miss Rabbit, I wondered if you would like to accompany me on my tour, as my assistant. If Eliza can spare you.'

'Well, I suppose I there's not much for her to do around here while the building work is happening. Is that what you want, dear?'

'Can Nelson come too?'

Faber nodded. 'If his family permit it.'

Nelson cheered, and Tig clapped her hands with joy.

'Only for the season, mind,' said Eliza. 'I'll need them back here when the theatre re-opens. Tig's got a lot of learning to do if she's going to be theatre manager one day.'

Tig threw her arms around Eliza who hugged her tightly. 'I'll miss you very much. And the Royale.'

'I will understand if you don't want to leave,' said Faber, looking concerned.

'I do,' said Tig. 'I want to go. And anyway, you'll need our help if Euphonia starts talking on her own again.'

But she never did.

Author's Note

In 1848, Tig's Manchester was crowded, noisy, and expanding fast.

Vast mills worked day and night. Deafening and dangerous machinery spun raw cotton into threads and wove them into fabric to be sold all over the world. Less than a hundred years earlier, these jobs had been done by hand. Now huge steam powered contraptions were taking over, and people flocked to the cities in their thousands to find work in the mills.

The people of Manchester were compared to worker bees, swarming in and out of the mills, always busy, always working, tiny parts of a vast hive of industry. Look closely in Manchester today and you'll find bees hidden everywhere – a symbol of Manchester's proud and difficult industrial history.

As the mill owners got rich, the people who actually did the work had hard, short lives. Days were long, wages were low, and health and safety was non-existent. Poor people lived in awful conditions – whole families in a single room and whole streets sharing one outdoor toilet.

Factories were not the only places taking advantage of new inventions. Theatre machinery made actors fly above the stage and disappear through the floor. The introduction of gas lighting allowed them to make shows more spectacular than ever. The 1840s saw the beginning of magic shows and stage illusions. Inventors made amazing automata – complicated clockwork toys that could do difficult actions like walking, dancing or even writing.

It was against the backdrop of this world of magic and machinery that the real Joseph Faber and his incredible talking machine arrived in England. In our world of computers and AI, it's hard to imagine how groundbreaking his invention was. Years before the first sound recordings were made, if you wanted to hear a song, you had to go to a show, or sing it yourself. Telephones were still decades away – no one had ever heard a voice from a machine before. Euphonia was incredibly sophisticated, and Faber had spent years perfecting her.

Unfortunately for Professor Faber, audiences hated her. Euphonia's voice was flat and unnerving – one witness wrote that it sounded like a voice from the depths of a tomb. Her face was realistic, but only her lips and tongue moved, which audiences found creepy. Faber was a genius but not much of a performer. He was said to look untidy, even haunted, and to be completely obsessed with his invention.

Though Faber never got the credit he deserved, some people did recognize how special Euphonia was. One was American scientist Joseph Henry, who played a big part in inventing the telegraph (the first machine that could send electronic messages over long distances). He thought the two inventions could be combined, so a message sent by telegraph would be spoken by the talking machine at the other end.

Another notable fan was Melville Bell, who studied how speech is produced and found Faber's work inspiring. You may have heard of his son, Alexander Graham Bell, who invented the telephone. Lucky for us he did, or we might have mechanical talking heads in our living rooms instead . . .

Turn the page for an enthralling
extract of the critically–acclaimed
THE VANISHING TRICK

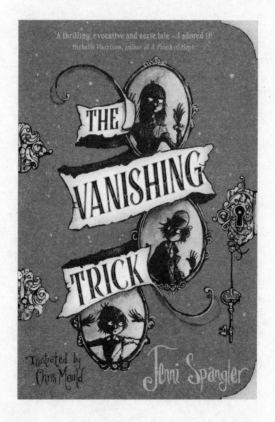

'A thrilling, evocative and eerie tale – I adored it!'
Michelle Harrison

1
The Fool:
Beginnings,
Fearlessness, Folly

LEANDER

It wasn't a sin to steal if you only took forgotten things.

Leander had been watching the ugly mutton pie in the bakery window for hours. It was lopsided and slightly squashed. All day customers had ignored it in favour of plump loaves, golden apple pies and sugar-sprinkled shortbread. The pie was left alone, unwanted and forgotten.

Leander knew how that felt.

Lurking by the doorway, he breathed in hot, sweet air each time someone went inside and his stomach ached with emptiness. The evening grew dark and people rushed along the cobbles, pulling coats and shawls tight to keep out the chill. Nobody would buy the pie now.

Wastefulness was a sin, too, and Leander was so hungry.

He had tried to find work, but nobody wanted to hire a scruffy orphan with no schooling and no one to vouch for his character. Every now and then, he'd earn a few coppers for a day of labour. Last week he'd spent two days mucking out a pig shed – horrible, cold, smelly work – only for the woman to say his work wasn't up to snuff, and short him half his money. Since then, nothing. People always thought he was up to no good – even when he wasn't. So, if he wanted to eat, he usually had to steal. Honesty and hunger were in constant competition for his soul and today hunger was winning.

Peering through the steam-clouded glass, Leander waited for the wiry baker to turn his back, then darted in. He snatched the pie, shoved it into his pocket and ran.

'Oi!'

The baker was after him. Leander sprinted up the high street, pushing between two men in top hats and dodging an old lady with a cane. He darted across the road, narrowly missing the wheels of a carriage.

'Whoa there!' shouted the driver.

'Thief!' the baker cried, still on Leander's heels.

Leander scrambled over a wall and rounded a corner. If he was caught, he'd get a thrashing or worse – be taken before the law. He dashed into an alley, his panicked footsteps sending rats skittering from their hiding places in the shadows.

Up ahead, warm light spilled from low windows. The inn.

If he was fast and clever, he could lose his pursuer in the crowded alehouse. He shoved the door open, breathless, heart pounding.

'Watch it, son—' He almost collided with a man carrying tankards.

'Sorry!' Leander hopped over the legs of a sleeping drunk and squeezed between tables. Lucky he was so small and skinny for his age. The air was stuffy-warm, heavy with tobacco smoke and the stale scent of old beer. He ducked beneath a man's arm and kicked an overturned chair out of his path.

The baker thundered in. The gaffer was fast.

Leander dropped to the sticky floor and crawled under tables, avoiding booted feet and puddles of drink. This was too close. He raced to the opposite corner and through the narrow black door that led to the adjoining coach house.

Cool night air washed over his flushed cheeks. The coach house was a cavernous room, with wooden beams and an earthy hay smell. The big barn doors were chained and bolted – no escape there. To his right was a row of horse stalls. Could he hide there? No, unsettled horses would give his location away.

Then he saw it. A pristine black carriage, empty and waiting patiently for its owner's return. Perfect. He yanked open the door and jumped inside.

The smell came first, dry and sharp, sour and musty all at once, like last autumn's rotten leaves after the snow melts, and old books, and pine tar, and spoiled meat.

Pots, pans and bundles of herbs hung from the ceiling, brushing against his ears. There was a bench on one side covered with dusty blankets and rugs. The other wall was fitted with dozens of wooden drawers and compartments, some gaping open, leaves and spoons and feathers poking out at all angles. Every other inch was covered with ramshackle shelves crammed with cards and papers and bottles of murky coloured liquids and – Leander leaned in to inspect the biggest jar – was that the skeleton of a rat? Why would anyone want such a thing?

A noise. Someone was here.

Footsteps click-clacked across the flagstones. Not the powerful gait of the baker. These were sure and sharp.

Stupid! He should have checked there was no one around. If he'd been seen climbing into the carriage, he was in bigger trouble than ever.

'Who's there?' a woman's voice called from the far corner. 'Who is in my carriage?'

Leander's heart raced. Whoever owned this collection of strange and eerie things wasn't a person he wanted to meet. He jumped out and darted behind a wooden post.

'What mischief is this?' the woman said.

Click, click, click.

The footsteps came closer, slower now but unhesitating. Blood pounded in Leander's head and he pressed his back against the post. His warm breath made white clouds in the cold air.

'Come out. I know you're there. I can smell you.'

Out of sight, horses shifted in their stalls, hooves scraping over straw and stone.

'Now then, don't be shy.' There was almost a laugh in the woman's voice. She paced round the carriage towards Leander's hiding place.

Beyond the inn door the muffled fury of the baker's voice grew louder. If Leander stayed put, the baker would see him the moment the door opened. But, if he ran for the back door, he'd collide with the carriage owner. He felt like a fox with hounds closing in on both sides.

Thinking quickly, he dived under the carriage, feeling the pie squish in his pocket as he rolled over and tucked himself behind the back wheel.

The inn door was flung open.

'When I get my hands on you—!' the baker roared, stopping abruptly as he noticed the woman. 'Beg pardon, ma'am. Did a boy come this way?'

Leander's chest tightened. Any moment now, he'd be dragged out and . . .

'No,' replied the woman. She stepped in front of the wheel and flicked out her dress, obscuring Leander's hiding place. 'I haven't seen anyone.' Leander could only see her ankles, but from her fancy blue dress and crisp speech he could tell she came from money.

'Been thieving. Yay high,' the man said, panting. 'Long hair, short trousers.'

'I assure you I'm quite alone.'

Leander was confused. Why would this woman lie for him?

'Right you are,' said the baker. 'Sorry to trouble you.'

'Not at all.'

'Sneaky little blighter. I've 'ad a few things go missing lately. First time I've seen who was responsible.'

'Is that so?' the woman said.

'Best keep an eye out, ma'am. He's a wrong'un.'

'Thank you, I shall.'

Leander held his breath as the baker's footsteps retreated. He listened for the *creak-thud* of the inn door closing.

'A thief, is it?' the woman said. 'Out with you, then.'

Not likely. Leander scrabbled away beneath the carriage and out the other side only to find the woman already looming over him. She was tall, with coal-black hair piled high beneath a peacock-green hat. Although she was beautiful, a coldness hung around her, more biting than the November air.

'Why were you in my carriage?' she asked, not unkindly.

'Wasn't.' He sidestepped to get round her, but she blocked his path.

'There's no need to lie, but you must explain yourself.'

The blue satin of the woman's dress brushed against his legs. Any closer and she'd be standing on his feet. He sized her up; something was unsettling. Why would this grand lady have a carriage full of feathers and bones and other oddities? And why would she save him from a beating from the baker . . . ?

'I wasn't doing anything.' He shrugged. 'Just looking round.'

'And if I should check your pockets?'

'Check them.' He raised his chin defiantly.

'Terrible things happen to liars and thieves, little boy.' Her voice was musical, her lips smiling.

Their eyes met and, for several seconds of hideous silence, Leander didn't dare look away. It seemed the woman could see every dark spot on his soul and every bad thing he had ever done.

'What's around your neck, child?' Her voice was still steady and calm. 'Something of mine?'

'No. Truly I didn't take anything.' The moment she looked away, he'd be out of there. She might have protected him, but he didn't trust this woman with her strange carriage. He desperately wanted to go somewhere safe and eat his pie.

'Come now, I won't hurt you. Show me.'

The woman stared at his throat like a wolf ready to bite. Leander pulled the locket from his grubby linen shirt. 'It was . . .'

'Your mother's,' she finished for him.

A pit opened in Leander's middle. 'How did you know?'

'Ah yes,' she whispered, a dreamy expression crossing her face. 'Now I see. A motherless child – an orphan, yes?'

Leander couldn't form words. What witchcraft was this?

'All alone in the world.' She stroked his cheek with the back of her hand, feather-light. 'Lost.'

He stuck out his chin. 'I can look after myself.'

'May I?' she asked, fingers already curling round the locket. She leaned in, the thick scent of lavender and violets smothering him. 'Interesting.'

He wriggled from her grip. 'I have to go.'

'You are miserable,' she said. 'I know a little about misery. I could help you.'

'Don't need help.' Leander knew she was just pretending to care so she could feel virtuous. He didn't want her pity.

Yes, he was alone, but that was fine. No one to let him down. People only cared about themselves.

She laughed. 'I think you do. You can trust me. You must be famished.'

Then again . . . Maybe if he played for sympathy she'd give him some money, or food. He could be nice, for a minute, and run if things went wrong.

'I collect trinkets, as you've seen.' She gestured towards the carriage.

Trinkets? A rat skeleton was hardly a trinket, but Leander bit his tongue.

'I'd be willing to buy your locket, as a kindness. It's clear you need the money.'

'Or you could just *give* me money.' He tried a cheeky smile.

'Impertinent little thing, aren't you?' She laughed. 'No. It must be a fair trade. No nonsense.'

Leander's mind whirred. He'd already pawned his mother's boots and coat, sold her pots and pans and even traded her bed sheets to the ragman. The locket was the last thing he had left. If he sold that, too, there would be nothing of hers to hold. It would be like she never existed. The thought made his eyes sting with tears. No. He couldn't part with it. He *wouldn't*. Then, as if reminding him of the reality of his situation, his stomach growled loudly. What choice did he really have? He had no other way to make money, and the more he stole, the more chance he'd be caught. Today had been a close call with the baker, but what happened when his luck ran out?

'It's not real gold,' said Leander. Should he . . . ?

'Indeed not. But I am a soft-hearted creature, and I've taken a liking to it.'

'I don't . . .'

'It would be hard to part with it, I'm sure,' she said. 'But your mother would understand. Do you think she'd rather you went hungry?'

And he was hungry. So hungry. Her words brought the ache back to his belly. The flattened mutton pie wouldn't fill him for long. Three days ago he'd spent his last penny on a pint of pea soup and a hot potato. Yesterday all he'd had were three bruised pears he'd swiped by climbing someone's garden fence. There was never enough food.

'Is the latch still intact? Does it open and close?' she asked.

Leander nodded. To go from being caught stealing to earning some honest money was a good turn of events, but his mother's locket . . . Could he?

'I'm sure I can find you a tempting sum. Shall we say ten shillings?'

Ten shillings! He couldn't remember when he last had a full shilling to his name.

Behind the woman, a girl appeared at the open carriage door. Leander blinked in surprise. Where had she come from? There had been no one inside a moment before . . . The girl put her finger to her lips, urging him to stay silent. Was she trying to steal something, too? No. She looked too neat and well dressed to be a street child. The woman's daughter perhaps? She looked about eleven, like Leander, and had the same dark hair as the woman.

'Six, seven, eight...' The woman counted coins from an embroidered pouch. 'What do you say, boy?'

The girl shook her head frantically and mouthed, 'No,' her expression a picture of panic.

The girl's urgency alarmed Leander back to his senses. He couldn't possibly sell the only thing he had left of his mother!

'No,' he said firmly.

The woman's face fell.

'It's very kind of you, miss, but I couldn't part with the locket.'

She stiffened up and scowled. 'A shame. If you change your mind, I shall be here until morning. Ask for Madame Pinchbeck.'

Was that it? She was letting him leave?

Leander glanced towards the girl. The movement alerted the woman, who spun round.

'How dare you?' She lunged towards the girl, who retreated into the carriage, the door slamming.

Leander took his chance and ran.

About the Author

Jenni Spangler writes children's books with a magical twist. She loves to take real and familiar places and events and add a layer of mystery and hocus-pocus. Her debut novel, *The Vanishing Trick*, was selected as Waterstones Children's Book of the Month and longlisted for the Branford Boase Award. *The Incredible Talking Machine* is her second book with Simon & Schuster Children's Books.

Jenni lives in Staffordshire with her husband and two children. She loves old photographs, picture books and tea, but is wary of manhole covers following an unfortunate incident.

www.jennispangler.com
Follow Jenni on Twitter @JenniSpangler1

About the Illustrator

Chris Mould is an award-winning illustrator who went to art school at 16. A sublime draftsman with a penchant for the gothic, he has illustrated a huge range of books, from picture books and young fiction, to theatre posters and satirical cartoons for national newspapers. His children's book work includes Matt Haig's bestselling Christmas titles, a reimagining of Ted Hughes' *The Iron Man* (shortlisted for the 2020 Kate Greenaway Medal) and a recently published illustrated *Animal Farm*.

Chris lives in Yorkshire with his wife, has two grown-up daughters, and when he's not drawing and writing, you'll find him… actually, he's never not drawing or writing.

chrismould.blogspot.co.uk
Follow Chris on Twitter @chrismouldink